MALUNGA AT WAR

NISSIH AGISHI OLABE

MALUNGA AT WAR

WRITTEN BY

NISSIH AGISHI OLABE

nissiholabe@gmail.com

Published by:

COMMUNE WRITERS INT'L
www.communewriters.com
+234 8139 260 389

Published in the Federal Republic of Nigeria

PROLOGUE

Long before time and seasons began, humans with great strength like the gods dwelled in a realm that looked just like the universe. They were powerful and did all kinds of evil. Babies were being slaughtered and their blood drunk like wine. Men lived like savages; a neighbour in the morning could be the next meal for dinner. The lawlessness was consuming and tiring.

Then arose Nyambe; a king who had witnessed enormous evil but now sought-after peace and tranquility. He was dissatisfied with how men lived and wanted rest, joy and peace. With his powers, he created the land of Malunga; a place in present-day East Africa, where no evil existed. It was a land of peace, a land where nature sat on its throne and beauty sprouted like the morning dew.

Malunga was a land where the sun rose over the horizon and splashed its beauty across the wildlife into the hearts of men. The soil was rich and succulent, giving birth to bountiful harvests and joyous celebration seasons.

Nyambe was not left without opposition, as Buwana, the three-horned and three-eyed demon, along with his two sons, tried to defy the purity of the heart of men by disrupting the peace of Malunga and instilling the agony of evil.

Nyambe and the guardian of peace, Ruhu, fought Buwana and his sons, breaking one of Buwana's horns before holding him captive in a large bottle for centuries in the Stone Wall of Secrets. This was where history was stored, in scrolls made from animal skin. Ruhu had been the guardian of all truth and was in charge of the prisoners until the unavoidable happened.

As the saying goes, evil always has a way of invading the land of humans, and Nyambe was not ignorant of this truth, just as Ruhu the guardian. However, who could have known the day evil would rise? Perhaps sooner than expected; or perhaps Buwana's one-eyed horn buried in the north of the Stone Wall of Secrets would have the answer to the coming contentions for the land of Malunga.

1

That night, the moon spread out like a blanket over the horizon of Malunga. There laid Princess Atama in the upper chambers next to her father, Nyambe. Though asleep, she remained restless. She woke up, took off her zebra bed cover and stood by the window. From there, she could see the woods, the fountain of peace, and the tower of the Stone Wall of Secrets at the north wing of the palace.

"The shadow.... I see shadows mingling in the dark. What could that be?"

She strained to see the creatures.

"Oh no!" That's Makundu, her brother, the prince and his boy servant, Masisi.

"Not again. What could they be up to at this time of the night? Aren't they ever tired of their adventures and experimentations? But they seem to be having fun. I wish I could join them, or maybe I should."

She looked over at Zuchi, her girl servant who was sleeping in a corner of the room. Noiselessly, she took her snake-skin cape and tiptoed out of the room, heading towards where she saw Makundu and Masisi.

"Masisi, look at what I found."

With pleasure, Makundu handed over the marble stone to his friend and servant. Masisi took the marble stone and admired it for a moment before tucking it into the hunter's bag of collections he carried, which housed all sorts of items they'd picked on different occasions.

The young teenage boys could navigate their way through the woods because of the full moon. So, they didn't worry about getting lost.

"What is that?" Masisi asked, pointing to a shiny blue object half buried in the soil.

"Let's dig it out and see," suggested Makundu.

They began to dig, using the tools from Masisi's bag. They dug and dug and soon pulled out a 10-inch horn with an eye.

"Wow, it's beautiful!"

Masisi peeped inside the horn and a strange smell consumed him. Taken aback, he shook his head to clear his vision before tucking the horn into the collection bag.

"We will examine it better tomorrow; let's go to the Stone Wall of Secrets," Masisi suggested.

"I'm not sure about that. It's late and Ruhu might be asleep by now. I'm sure he wouldn't like us roaming in there without his permission," Makundu noted.

"Let go now, I said!" Masisi commanded in an authoritative voice.

Taken aback by Masisi's tone, Makundu asked,

"Are you okay?"

Taking a hold of himself, he responded,

"Yeah, I'm okay. Sorry about my tone; I'm just having so much fun that I feel like we can have a little adventure without the watchful eye of Ruhu. You never can tell, it might be so much fun, please master."

"Okay, you only know how to cajole me into doing your will, especially when you call me master. You are my best friend, Masisi, and you know I will do anything for you. More so, you don't have to call me master, okay?" Makundu said.

"Yes, master," replied Masisi, playfully punching Makundu in the ribs before taking off towards the Stone Wall of Secrets. Makundu took off after him, with playful determination to catch up and teach him a good lesson.

Atama got to the spot she last saw those two, but found them laughing and running towards the Stone Wall of Secrets.

"What are they up to again, and why are they so excited?" she wondered. These boys are so adventurous!

"Oh! I wish I was a boy, then they would allow me to join them. Boys have so much fun. I dislike the long hours I have to sit for my thick afro hair to be braided, but I'd rather endure the braids than sit for hours making waist beads. I wish I was a boy, at least, I would be allowed to chase the buffalos, dive into the fountain of peace, climb trees, or go on adventures like Makundu and Masisi," Atama lamented.

Flinging her thoughts aside, she noiselessly ran after them.

Some minutes later, Zuchi woke up and couldn't find Princess Atama. She looked towards the window and saw Atama running towards the Stone Wall of secrets.

"Oh, Princess Atama! What are you doing by this time of the night? Surely the king will not be pleased if he finds out we are not in bed."

She chided herself as she planned to go after her.

She took her cape and tiptoed out of the palace.

"Look, there's a glow in the bag! The eye of the horn, let's take a look!" cried Makundu.

They brought out the horn and the glow reflected towards a particular direction. Quietly, they followed the lead of the glow down to a dungeon they never knew existed. Soon, they reached the source of the glow, it emanated from a giant bottle that housed a human creature. The strange creature had two horns with eyes on each, just like the one they held.

Gripped with fear and uncertainty, Makundu suggested, "Let's leave this place. It feels strange and I'm terrified."

Alas, it was too late as powers emanated from the bottle into the horn in Masisi's hands. The room was glowing and smoky. Makundu ran towards the stone entrance but couldn't find his way because the smoke blurred his vision.

***

"Who's there?" called out Ruhu, the guardian of the Stone Wall of Secret. Using his lamp, he checked the left-wing stairways.

"I know I heard footsteps," he thought.

"Zuchi! What are you doing here by this time of the night?"

"Forgive me, Ruhu; I only came after my mistress, the princess. I saw her heading this way a few minutes ago from the palace window. I have no intention of being here of my own accord. If you would allow me, I would fetch her and we would be on our way back to our chambers," Zuchi pleaded.

"Buwana!" Ruhu retorted, quickly running towards the dungeon where the bottled prisoners were kept. Zuchi ran after him confused.

"Is Princess Atama in danger?" She asked as they ran towards the dungeon.

***

"What have you done?" screamed Atama who had just walked in to witness the unbelievable.

Makundu lay on the floor in the pool of his blood; while Masisi held the one-eyed horn with fresh blood dripping from its tip.

"Hahaha!" laughed Masisi in the voice of Buwana. "Here comes another royal blood to feed on and to free one of you, sons. Victory has finally come to us."

He turned to one of his sons in the bottle and said, "I shall free you first."

"You wicked spirit, I rebuke you and forbid you from touching the royal blood," cried Ruhu whose eyes had turned blue. Fire proceeded out of his mouth.

"Not today, Ruhu. You know the rules. Back in the days when we ruled, no one could take lawful captives; it's forbidden! These are now my prey," Buwana declared.

Ruhu replied, "You can't have them. We do not operate by the rules from the dark world; our rules here say even the lawful captives shall be delivered."

Within seconds, fire came out of Ruhu's mouth and snatched Atama from Buwana's firm grip. It shielded Zuchi and he took the corpse of prince Makundu.

Buwana raged with a loud voice and the entire kingdom of Malunga heard it, for the battle line had been drawn.

"Buwana is back!" gasped Nyambe from the chambers of his palace.

"Where are Makundu and Atama? Where is Ruhu, the guardian of the Stone Wall of Secrets?"

Before he could use his powers to seek the truth, Ruhu sent a magical signal through his signet ring, revealing the scenario to him. Nyambe was heartbroken as he visualized his son being murdered in cold blood by the powers of Buwana. He knew that the day of evil would surely come, but to think that Buwana would kill his son without thinking twice meant that the battle line had indeed been drawn. He was relieved that Ruhu was at the outer court and knew what to do. First, he must proceed to safeguard the palace and Princess Atama. His bloodline must fight and defeat the evil Buwana, and restore Malunga from the fist of evil, thus restoring peace to the kingdom.

Nyambe communicated with Ruhu saying;

"The destiny of purity and peace is now saddled on her shoulders, else, humanity will be doomed under the powers of evil and Buwana will reign forever. You know how to find me when the time comes, but for now, you must take the lead and show her the way. I will be waiting on the other side."

With that, Nyambe vanished together with the palace into the unknown, along with the corpse of Prince Makundu. The servants and everyone residing in the palace at the time also vanished with him. The Stone Wall of Secrets became invisible as well.

They all hid in the big ancient oak tree for days. Ruhu tried to explain to Atama the seriousness of the war at hand and the implications of losing it, but Atama was in so much grief for losing everything; first her brother, then her father. From living in the palace to hiding in a big oak tree, the whole thing was scary.

"We must get to the other side of the river before sunset. When we cross the river, we leave Malunga. I must prepare you for the battle and we must send arrows from without. That way, we are sure of subduing evil and restoring the good of Malunga," Ruhu assured Atama.

2

The night was setting and unfolding the morning clouds. At cockcrow, Ruhu woke the ladies.

"Atama, wake up; Zuchi, it's time we started moving."

The horizon smelt of doom and the clouds seemed guilty of holding a secret. They started the journey but Atama was slow and dragged her feet unenthusiastically, mostly from deep grief and lack of interest to survive the day.

"Hasten up, Atama; we need to find the river before the demon-possessed Masisi finds us," cried Ruhu.

Atama made no effort to speed up, nor did she respond. Her lack of interest and indifference were frustrating but no one complained because a girl of her age had no business harbouring grief after such great losses in a day. What she didn't realize were the supernatural powers that lay within her soul.

"If only she could reach her inner self; even her sorrows could become bearable," Ruhu thought quietly.

Ruhu possessed the ability to read minds, amongst other superpowers. He had laid fallow his powers for long, having no use for them except as the guardian of the Stone Wall of Secrets. Now he must resurrect his powers for the battle ahead and must reveal the true nature of Atama to her in due time.

"Hush!" Ruhu made a fist to halt the girls, "I hear a sound. It's coming our way with a speed of 3km per second. I perceive we won't be able to cross the river before they get here."

Taking Zuchi's shoes off her feet, Ruhu exchanged them with Atama's. He touched them at the same time and an incredible thing happened; their attires were switched, making Atama the maid and Zuchi the princess. Before Atama could open her mouth to complain, Ruhu had touched her forehead and her memory was wiped, just before the net of Masisi caught them all in a web.

"You think I will let you slip off my hands with the princess who is the access to regaining what was stolen from me? Ruhu, you have cost me much and I shall repay you handsomely," came the enemy's voice.

They were taken away with Atama who was already perplexed. She became more confused about the turn of events as they rode back as captives.

"Zuchi, you will play your part as the princess in the open, but in secret, you must attend to Atama as your mistress," Ruhu instructed.

He could hear the raging thoughts of confusion in Atama's head.

"What am I doing here?" She wondered in a state of blankness. "I have been captured; I need to get away from them all, and this is not my home."

Compassion washed over Ruhu seeing her that way, but he had to do it, lest her true identity be revealed and the mission thwarted.

"My dear, take some rest and be at peace. This is a temporary situation; we will all be safe and free soon."

"And who are you?" She thought silently. Why is a prisoner like me speaking words of peace and reassurance? Can't he see we are all prisoners?"

"The mind is the greatest prison and not this temporal cage," Ruhu said in response to her thoughts.

She said nothing but closed her eyes and surrendered to the powers of sleep.

"I must help her find herself again. She must learn the power of her mind. That way, she will reconnect with her true self and find the will to carry her cross," Ruhu thought.

***

Masisi assembled the people of Malunga to admonish them.

"People of Malunga, you're all mine now. I'm your king and I expect total allegiance. I shall rend down this place and set my throne on high. I shall rule over the world and will not tolerate any opposition."

"Our allegiance is to Nyambe, our true king," someone retorted from the crowd and the rest responded in agreement.

"Hush, you god-forsaken wretch!" Masisi said, as his eyes turned red. He stretched out his hands and they became elongated until they fetched the speaker from the crowd.

"Then, go join Nyambe your dead king in his grave." In a second, he slit the throat of the speaker before the crowd who gasped in fear and wonder, for they had never seen such evil.

"Any other challenge? I will gladly attend to it," cried Masisi, but no one dared raise a voice or lift a finger against the evil power before them.

"Don't worry, I am better off than your weak king; you will soon see. He has kept you away from a lot of good things. He has turned your mind to that of little babes, but I will show you real power, strength, and glory. You shall see and become gods. I shall bestow you with unsearchable knowledge and strength. Together, we shall build kingdoms and systems," Masisi bragged.

In no time, Masisi, via the powers of Buwana, established his kingdom. He raised an army far more numerous than the sand on the seashore. He rolled away the green vegetation of Malunga and set a blanket over the sun, lifting an eye as a star to light up his kingdom. The forest was trampled upon and a new throne was set up. The glory of Malunga rolled away and a new system began.

However, for Masisi to sit on the throne with a legitimate crown and gain all the powers of Malunga, he must find where Nyambe has vanished and gain access to the signet ring and all its powers. This means subduing Nyambe and placing him, his son and his daughter into the giant bottle in exchange for the freedom of Buwana's sons. That way, good will be lost, and this time, it will be forever. He was going to use Atama, the princess and Ruhu, the guardian to achieve his goal.

The citizens of Malunga were not spared as the hard labour soon began. They were made to work with metals and irons, other than the stones they were accustomed to. They were constantly hungry and tired. The land was getting stubborn and there was not enough sun or rain to bring bountiful harvests. The new king demanded they paid huge taxes. Their wives were taken away from them and their children were also forced into labour. The men soon became angry and bitter, harbouring and conceiving evil in their hearts against their fellow humans. They stole from one other, killed for bread and had illicit sex to find relief from the daily hardship.

Nevertheless, a small percentage of the people did not pledge their allegiance to the powers of Buwana. Ruhu the guardian began to search for clean hearts through mind reading and was able to pick a handful of them who hadn't bowed to the powers of Buwana, hoping that Nyambe would save them soon. Ruhu tried to keep their hopes alive and help them not to surrender, and to hold on to their faith in Nyambe.

The prisoners were kept in an open cell with the ground covered with straws and hay. A young guard in his early twenties, not far from Atama's age, was in charge of them.

"You have a great deal to learn if you must accomplish the mission. Remember, the future of Malunga is in your hands, Atama." Ruhu was whispering to a confused and indifferent lady.

"See, I'm tired of this talk of saving the world and defeating the devil. Hey Mr.... I'm trying to understand who I am. Everything looks strange and confusing. I can't even remember my name," Atama lamented.

"Atama. Your name is Princess Atama of Malunga, daughter of the great King Nyambe," came the response immediately.

"Okay, that's it. Now you add princess to my name, and who is Nyambe? Why is he not here to save me, to rescue us all if he is a great king as you claim? You call me a princess and then you say I'm the maid to her,"

Atama said, pointing at Zuchi who was sitting quietly with her head bowed.

Ruhu was quiet for a moment, allowing her to rend her frustration and complaints. He understood her absolutely but couldn't help her. He must do what he had to do, to shield her from herself and the grief while teaching her about her identity and the powers that lay within her. Buwana was very powerful and experienced; he had been existing for centuries. Atama was just a baby with powers beyond her comprehension. However, those same powers would ruin her and bring the mission to a total defeat if not properly used, and it surely would be a total disaster if Masisi got hold of the powers.

He would have to keep trying but didn't know how long until she will comply and start her training. There's a price to be paid for every minute wasted, but patience must have its full course for the mission to be flawlessly executed.

Zuchi wondered what would become of her and prayed silently that Atama would eventually listen to Ruhu and save them all, although her life and allegiance would forever be to Nyambe and the kingdom of Malunga.

The next day at sunrise, two guards dragged the prisoners from their sleep and brought them before Masisi. One of the young guards forced them to their knees before Masisi, who was sitting on a throne. The throne was made of bones and a skull, with the top having a long horn with an eye on it.

“I see you are enjoying my reign already,” Masisi’s crocked voice echoed in the room.

“Now I demand you pledge your allegiance to me as king or face the consequences. Oh, let me show you what the consequences look like,” Masisi said as he sent for a breast-feeding mother with her six months old baby to be brought from one of the cells where he kept the rebels.

A tall, slim and dark young woman, with her wailing baby, stood before Masisi. The baby was taken from her. With a punch, she was forced to go on her knees. Masisi rose from his one-eyed throne of skulls and headed her way. The child kept wailing in anxiety and discomfort.

Turning to the woman he said,

"I will only ask once; are you ready to deny your weak King Nyambe and pledge your allegiance to me, declaring the power of Buwana as the ultimate?"

"Please, Masisi. Please, don't hurt my child. I beg you in the name of our true King Nyam…"

Before she could complete her sentence, the head of her baby rolled down before her very eyes. The woman went crazy with rage and charged towards Masisi with her purple eyes emanating fire and revenge. With a snap of the finger, Masisi quenched the fire and bore his nails into her neck.

The woman's last words were "evil can only thrive for a while, but when she is ready, she will crush your head and bruise your heel until you are back into the bottle forever."

In annoyance, Masisi squeezed her neck until it shrieked and her body lay like a rag on the floor.

"Bitch!" He called out.

"I shall have no mercy on my victims and my prey shall know no escape," he yelled in a rage, turning to the wide-eyed onlookers.

"Now, you will denounce Nyambe and pledge your allegiance to me as king, and the powers of Buwana as ultimate.

A teary-eyed Zuchi turned towards Ruhu and began to plead that he saved them. Atama was scared but realized an uncontrollable anger surging out of her, with a strange desire to strangle the head of this demon. The image of the dead child's head rolling on the floor and that of the dead woman blurred her teary eyes. She was filled with rage. Ruhu was aware of the turmoil in her heart. He needed to distract Masisi and stop Atama from revealing her powers, knowing she lacked the knowledge of controlling them.

"I will start with the princess," Masisi threatened as pointed at Zuchi to be brought forward.

"Now listen to me, you little soul. You will bow to me or I will skin you alive with my bare hands."

Immediately, Ruhu got into the mind of Atama and began to show images of her in a fierce battle with Masisi, until she defeated him and the powers of Buwana were tucked back into the bottle.

Her mind was calm but her body was weak from the imaginary combat, making her slump to the ground.

Ruhu then turned to Masisi who held a sharp knife, ready to skin Zuchi.

"But if you kill the princess, how do you plan to find the palace with Nyambe and the dead prince? Killing her means you will never free your two bottled sons, and your powers alone cannot bury good forever or prevail against the return of Nyambe. Meanwhile, you know what he will do when he returns. He shall avenge the death of his son by crushing you beyond recognition before sending you back into the everlasting bottle, and I shall be glad to guard you forever."

"Shut up! Shut up! You god-forsaken guardian," he fumed, flinging Zuchi who fell like a tornado against the wall before hitting the ground half-conscious.

"I will let her live, but I promise that I find the palace and when I meet Nyambe, I will do all that you have said to him. First, I shall skin the princess and suck the blood from her vagina before bottling her in exchange for my son, right before his very eye. As for you, I shall make you the guardian of their sufferings while you are in pain."

"Now get out of my presence while I think of how best to make use of you all," Masisi ordered.

Ruhu was thrown back into the straw cell, with Princess Atama and Zuchi dragged by their hair and thrown unceremoniously into the cell. The young guard doubled the cell's chains as he now knows the importance of the prisoners and what their escape would mean; 'death by his own hands'.

Hours later, Ruhu had gotten into the mind of Zuchi, drawing her back to consciousness, and she gasped as she opened her eyes.

"Water," she said.

Ruhu gave her a sip, then told her to rest while he treated her bruises with his healing powers.

Soon, they were both kneeling before Atama who was still unconscious and drained from the imaginary battle.

Ruhu held her hands and asked Zuchi to sing a lullaby close to her ears. Zuchi gladly complied.

"The stars are so beautiful,

The moon is so bright,

But their beauty comes from the great sun,

Fly with me that we may reach the source of the light,

Fly with me that it may shine through the darkness,

Fly with me that it may shield us from the coldness of fear,

Fly with me that we may smile forever."

The song was so soothing and beautiful that Ruhu found himself relaxing his head against the wall with his eyes closed. Even the young guard found himself drowsy from the sweet melody.

Atama opened her eyes.

"Where am I? The demon needs to stay in the bottle forever," she declared in a rage.

"Relax, dear one," Ruhu said, placing a hand on her forehead. "Soon, you will crush him and put him where he belongs, my dear".

She looked at Ruhu for a moment. Suddenly, the image of the child and the mother in cold blood flooded her vision. She turned to him, grabbing him fiercely by the arm.

"Teach me. Teach me all that there is to learn, teacher. Tell me all about my identity. I want to crush the enemy of my soul. Only then shall I find peace."

Ruhu smiled with satisfaction, looked at Zuchi and said,

"She is ready to take her path."

"I shall teach you, my dear."

She said nothing. However, her eyes spoke of her gratitude and determination.

Ruhu added,

"About that peace, you will find it from within, not from the vengeance of your enemy. Only then will you defeat your enemy from the point of victory and find freedom. Else, you differ not from the enemy himself."

She did not understand what he meant but decided to keep it in mind, to ask him later. She closed her eyes and buried her breath in the arms of deep sleep.

3

The Kingdom of Malunga kept drowning in the shackles of evil. Death and dread lay on the horizon. The once peaceful and promising atmosphere had thickened with the smell of human flesh and bloodshed, and the citizens were becoming savages.

Masisi had raised a ferocious army; fierce and terrible to behold. Those who had refused to pledge their allegiance to Buwana were kept in a dark attic and executed daily. Most of them hide in the woods, caves, and underground holes to save their lives while hoping that Nyambe would rescue them someday. They were aware of the survival of the princess; Ruhu constantly fed their minds with visions of Buwana's powers being defeated and Nyambe coming back to rescue them from the shackles of evil. All these birthed within them the hope and determination to rebel more against Masisi's reign.

The people had a flicker of hope, although from time to time, the remnant surrendered when they witnessed the brutal and merciless execution of one of them.

Those who had pledged their allegiance were not exempted from the harsh maltreatment of soldiers nor were they spared from the edge of the sword. A thief's hands were chopped off the other day and another thief was handed over for hungry crocodiles to feast on.

The rules were endless and the punishment for defaulting was unthinkable. No one was free and everyone lived in deep fear and dread.

In the cool of the evening, Ruhu would use his power to go around the city, scouting the minds of people to find the remnant, to encourage the hopeless and to reaffirm the powers and return of Nyambe. He also checked out the situation of things to ascertain how much time they had left.

Ruhu wasted no time in starting the training with Atama.

"I shall begin by telling you who you are. Never forget, you are Princess Atama, the existing heir of King Nyambe, and the blood for justice runs through your veins. Your father, the king is mighty, powerful and undefeatable but he plays by the rules; he is the just king. This war is about evil against good and evil cannot defeat you unless you assume the position of defeat. Though your skin is as soft as a feather, you are a warrior and your power is beyond comprehension. However, you must discover it yourself as you journey along, because good plays by the rules," Ruhu told Atama.

"What are the rules?" she asked.

"They lie in your path and you shall know them as you pursue your cause. Nevertheless, remember, there lies in your heart the abundance of truth. You must let it truly lead you," came Ruhu's response.

"So, what is my mission?" Curiosity made Atama ask.

"Use the power of truth to defeat Buwana. Send him back into the bottle and restore the glory of Malunga. Then shall the palace return and the reign of Nyambe be established forever. Masisi will be searching for the signet ring, which is believed to be hidden in dark secrets. It is the key to evoke Nyambe's realm and he must not find it."

"First, you shall learn servanthood. You must learn to serve Zuchi as the princess while you take the position of her maid, else Masisi will kill you both when he finds out," Ruhu cautioned the princess.

From then on, Zuchi took up the assignment of training Atama in the role and duties of a maid.

"When you stand as a maid, you must take a bow." Zuchi demonstrated, and Atama followed suit.

"Now, always keep your head bowed and do not speak until you are told to. Never make eye contact; it's a sign of boldness that isn't necessary for a maid. Also, remember to mind your business at all times," Zuchi added.

"Now let's practice the whole lesson from the beginning," said Zuchi.

Two weeks later, Masisi decided to make the princess his queen, planning to use subtlety to gain her trust. That way, he could use her as a key to achieving his aim. Therefore, he took Zuchi and placed her on a throne next to his, commanding that she should be treated well and be given all that she needed.

Zuchi assumed the throne as Masisi's queen while Princess Atama served as her maid.

All things worked as planned. Atama remembered to bow and stay heads down before the queen at all times. She cleaned and even scrubbed the floor. She combed and braided the queen's hair. She also stood laboriously for long hours attending to the queen.

Zuchi seemed pleased with her new position. At first, she was uncomfortable, seeing her dear friend and mistress bowing to her, but with the glory and power that came with the position of queen, Zuchi soon discovered that she enjoyed being served. It wasn't bad after all.

With Zuchi as queen, no attention was given to Atama. Therefore, she had ample time with Ruhu for further training.

Ruhu was made a gardener in the palace. When he is done with his work, he would teach Atama riddles, history and stories from the scrolls stored in his mind since the Stone Wall of Secrets was still yet to be found. He would close his eyes, go into the stonewall, and would begin to retrieve different scrolls and teach Atama from their contents.

Picking a scroll from a shelf, he said, "Let us learn the power of the mind."

"Close your eyes and close your mind also," Ruhu commanded.

"Shut out every distraction, both internal and external." Atama did as she was told.

"Now, open your mind's eye and see. Look deeply and you will see." Atama tried.

"I see nothing, Ruhu."

"Don't struggle to see, just see."

"But how? All I see is darkness."

"Yes, you have seen well. Now, find your path through the darkness. There shall you truly see the path within."

More confused than ever, Atama opened her eyes in dissatisfaction, picked up her snake-skinned cape, and left in rage without uttering a word.

4

Masisi stayed awake all night, consulting dark powers for access to the signet ring. In the palace, there was a section designed for his diabolical purposes which contained different evil articles - scrolls, calabash, candles and algae of different colours (green, red, and purple). After intense consultations with no result, he became frustrated and furiously commanded the guards to drag Ruhu to him immediately. Ruhu was still awake, as though expecting to be summoned.

He was taken from his cubicle in the lower chambers.

"You are the great guardian of the Stone Wall of Secrets. I'm sure you can reveal where to find the signet ring." Masisi thundered.

“You know it is impossible to find the signet ring. It doesn’t exist in this realm. Wherever Nyambe is, only there will you find it,” Ruhu responded.

“Ahhh, Ruhu! You said nothing is impossible unto him that believes, and I believe. Also, whoever seeks, surely shall he find. Therefore, I shall know no rest until I find the signet ring, and you are going to help me find it.”

“How? I have already told you it is not within my powers.”

“Yes, but the scrolls have always been in your possession. You will use your powers to access them for me, every single one of them. There lies the secret, and therein will the mystery be unveiled.”

“What you ask for is difficult. I cannot evoke ten thousand scrolls at once, especially in this atmosphere. The evil here is too much of a distraction for my mind.”

“And who said we will be doing it here? We shall take some soldiers along and ride to the mountains, far away from Malunga. There shall we find the right place. You shall evoke all the scrolls into several animal skins. If you try to be mischievous, the sharp edge of my horn driving through your heart will be the last thing you'll ever feel. We shall wait for as long as it takes, but we shall accomplish the mission."

Ruhu had no time to bid Atama farewell, for he was whisked away that night.

***

"Knock! Knock! Knock!" Atama knocked on Ruhu's door when she didn't see him in the garden that morning. She wondered if he was sick.

"But does Ruhu ever get sick or tired?" She wondered. Sometimes, she feels he is superhuman, other times, she thinks he is deific.

Anyway, she had to see him, considering how their last lesson went. Although she was sickened by the outcome, she was more disappointed in her failures. She had decided to try again, this time more determined to get it right as time was not a luxury.

She checked the window and could see his bed empty. When she tried the doorknob, the door opened. She went in and checked, but he wasn't there.

"Where could he be?" She wondered aloud.

Later, Atama found Zuchi sitting by the window in her chambers. She bowed in greeting.

"Come on, Princess Atama, you don't have to put on the act when we are alone."

"Ah! My lady, I'm already used to it and besides, it doesn't take away a thing from me, nor does it add to it. It makes me feel more human," the princess stated.

"Really?" Zuchi could not help but ask.

Zuchi could not comprehend that but did not linger on it.

Atama sat on the bed while Zuchi came to sit beside her.

"You look troubled, what's the matter?" Zuchi asked.

"It's Ruhu, I can't find him. I checked his chambers but he was not there. Do you have any slightest idea where he might be?"

Raising her brow for a moment, Zuchi exclaimed;

"Ah! Last night, from my window, I saw them ride away with some guards and they were fully armed. I think Masisi has taken him away. I hope he doesn't intend to kill him."

Atama was saddened. Her heart was in turmoil and she was afraid Masisi might kill him, knowing exactly what that would mean. She needed him because there was no way the mission could be accomplished without his help.

"I must find him." Atama turned to Zuchi.

"Are you sure about that? It's dangerous out there and you do not know the way they went, although I saw them go through the city."

"I must find him. I need him, the mission needs him, and besides, he might be in trouble. I must come to his rescue."

"I shall come with you then. If you must go, then we shall go together."

"Oh no! I don't think it's a good idea. Besides, the throne needs your crown and it will be suspicious if we both go missing. You must stay here and keep an eye on things, I'm the maid here, remember? Besides, no one will care if I'm gone or dead."

With that, she prepared herself immediately and went through the direction that she was told they had followed.

Atama did not believe the ruins in the city. This was her first time going through the city since it was captured by Masisi. The powers of Buwana had rendered the place desolate. There were soldiers everywhere, tormenting the citizens with all kinds of weapons. She could see women being flogged with whips openly on the streets. Curses and insults were hurled like rains of hay. The city reeked of blood and human flesh. The scene was devastating.

"Hey, look where you are going, you little brat."

An angry soldier spat those words at her in irritation. He shoved her aside, while a thin-looking man who was pushing the soldier's cart also hurled insults at her. His pain and outrage were birthed out of frustration due to her obstruction, causing him more pain.

She quickly jumped aside and hid in the crowd gathering at a corner close to the city gate.

A woman was shouting and begging for her life, while two merciless soldiers threw countless punches and kicks at her.

The crowd was increasing in number. The soldiers kept throwing punches at her. When her cries had seized, the soldiers thought she was dead. They took her body outside the city and dumped it along with several corpses and skeletons.

Atama closed her eyes in deep sadness, telling herself to be calm and focused. She stayed for about a minute or two, just to calm herself. She tried to look within to find peace. She opened her mind's eye to the same darkness she had experienced with Ruhu, but as she was about to shut her mind and open her physical eyes, she saw the woman who had been beaten and left to die outside the gate.

Although she wasn't at the gate yet, she could see the woman clearly as if she was standing right in front of her. Then the most shocking thing happened; she heard the woman's inner voice pleading for help.

"Who will help my daughter? I need help. I can't die. Oh! Please, I'm dying, but my daughter, she's only three. Please help! Nyambe, where are you? Where are you?"

The woman lamented in her heart.

Atama was more amazed than afraid that she could see and hear the thoughts of this woman. She wanted to shout and scream for joy. She wanted to run to Ruhu and tell him that she had found the right path in the darkness, but then she remembered that she was on a mission to find and rescue Ruhu. And then this helpless woman needs her help before she can continue on her mission.

The clouds had gathered, as it was about to rain. People were beginning to find shelter. She rushed to the gates and there she saw the woman, panting for her life.

She looked around but no one was in sight. So, she bent over and touched her, looking for her pulse, to ascertain if she was still alive.

"Excuse me, I'm here to help you. Do not be afraid."

Atama assured the helpless woman. She was in too much pain to hear or comprehend what Atama was saying because she was almost unconscious. Atama decided to try again.

"*Ma'ale* (mother), can you hear me?" Still, there was no sound. Then she decided to try communicating through the mind.

"*Ma'ale* (mother), can you hear me?"

"Help me. Don't let me die here. Help my daughter," came the woman's heart cry.

"*Rebutu, Ina wale chiko dim anam* (don't worry, your daughter will not die), let me help you first to safety, then we can find your daughter."

She helped the woman into the woods, and in no time, they found a cave. She laid her there and began nursing her. She took out the jar of water she hung by her waist and gave the woman a drink.

"*Kwenu, kwenu,* (drink, drink)," she forced her mouth open and poured some quantity down her throat.

She cleaned up the injuries, took out some ointment from her backpack and applied it to the injuries. The woman fell into a deep sleep.

When night came, Atama made a fire to keep them warm. Later that night, she was awakened by the woman's groan.

Atama touched her forehead to feel her temperature.

"Oh no! You're burning with fever."

She brought out a small bottle, got a bowl, heated a small quantity of water, and added two drops of the content from the bottle.

Sitting the woman upon her lap, she said, "*kwenu, kwenu* (drink, drink)."

She forced it into her mouth, down her throat, until the bowl was empty. Almost immediately, the woman went back to sleep.

"You look much better, how are you feeling today?" She asked when the woman woke up the next morning.

Atama had prepared another concoction for her, but first, she served her a piece of bread and water before giving her the hot brew. By noon, the woman was feeling a lot better and the fever was completely gone.

"*Utambga,* (thank you)", she said hours later after Atama gave her the last dosage of the concoction.

"You look a lot better; you will live," Atama added.

"*Utambga,* (thank you)," she said again.

"My daughter, I need to find her. Please, help me find her. She's only three and she must have eaten the last bread I gave her before leaving the house. I told her I would be back soon."

Wearing a sad face, she continued,

"She will cry all night and will be afraid of the dark. *Sisir* (Please help me)."

"Yes, I will find her. *Rebutu, ina wale chikozimkurbe* (don't worry, your daughter would be found). Now tell me, where is your house?"

The woman looked blank as if she could not remember.

For a while, she thought but still could not figure it out.

"How do I describe the hideout to her?"

Atama heard the woman's thoughts loud and clear, then decided to converse with her through the mind.

A thought came to her mind, then she asked the woman,

"Do you mind thinking about where your house is and I will follow the direction from your mind?"

The woman began to locate the hideout they called home. She moved until she stopped at a building that looked like an abandoned bakery. Inside the bakery, there was a wooden cabinet. It served as a door to a small room previously used as a store. No one would ever imagine it was a shelter. Therefore, no one cared to look or bother to pry into that location.

Having seen the place, Atama decided to look further. She was surprised to find a little dark-skinned girl sleeping with one of her hands wrapped around a dirty-looking rubber doll, while the thumb of the other hand was in her mouth. Her face was stained with dried tears. Atama's heart went all out for the three-year-old and she knew she would find no rest until she brought the girl to safety.

"I will go and get her right away," she said as she turned to the woman.

"*Utambga* (thank you)," the woman responded with many expressions of gratitude.

“Please keep still and rest. By the time you awake, your little one will be in your arms.” With that, Atama headed back into the city to find the girl.

By the time she got to the gate, the soldiers had brought two more bodies and dumped them outside the city gate, along with other corpses. No one noticed or cared about the absence of the woman’s body. She passed in silence, deliberately shutting her mind, lest she found another helpless soul amongst the corpse seeking her help.

She entered the city and began to use her mind to locate the old bakery. She passed a garbage dump site with rotten vegetables emanating a strong pungent smell. Two kids of about nine and twelve were scavenging, obviously for something to eat. She felt stomach cramps as she saw one of them grab something wrapped in animal skin to eat. It must have been rotten but they shared it and almost got into a fistfight when one of the boys felt he was cheated in the sharing.

Her heart went out to them; poor children.

"See what they have become!"

She soon began to lament in her mind, saying,

"Paying allegiance to Masisi doesn't guarantee your safety. You are as vulnerable as the resistance and you are not exempted from the hardship either."

Atama soon located the bakery. She entered but did not find anyone.

Afraid the girl was not there, she looked around but the girl was nowhere to be found. Remembering that she had not asked for the child's name and did not even ask the woman for her name, Atama felt lost and confused.

"What will I do now? I pray she's still alive. What if the soldiers heard her crying and took her away? Oh no! Please may it not be so."

She closed her eyes to think for a while, then came the darkness and she looked deeper and began to hear the sound of a child laughing. She followed the sound of the laughter which led her out of the house to the backyard. There she saw a little dark girl with an unkempt short ponytail, chasing after a kitten and laughing all the way.

Atama snapped from the vision, ran to the back of the old bakery, and there she was, playing with a kitten with a carefree attitude. She did not care or worry about a thing, not even the mucus flowing down her nostrils and dripping occasionally into her mouth. She immediately approached the child.

"*Loko!* (Hello!)," she said, stretching her hands in greetings. The child looked at her suspiciously for a while before answering,

"*Lokomala,* (hello aunty)."

"Is that your kitten?" Atama asked, pointing at the small kitten wrapped under the girl's armpit.

With much joy and enthusiasm, the child began to tell her all about the kitten.

"She's my best friend after *Ma'ale* (mother). She can play but doesn't talk. I found her when I came out to pee. *Ma'ale* (mother) said 'don't come out,' but I got pressed. *Ma'ale* (mother) said 'go out when you want to pee,' and *Ma'ale* (mother) said 'don't pee on the bed.' I tell *Ma'ale* (mother) 'I didn't pee on the bed' but *Ma'ale* (mother) will be sad I played outside."

"Don't worry, I'm sure *Ma'ale* (mother) will understand you had to go out to pee so as not to wet the bed."

The child was not sure but did not say anything. She was so excited to tell someone about her new friend that she did not give much thought to what Atama said.

"Look," she continued, showing Atama the claws of the kitten,

"I shared my bread with her. She was very hungry. I'm hungry too."

Then, as if she suddenly remembered that her mother was not back, she said as a tear escaped her eyes,

"*Ma'ale* (mother) went away and *Ma'ale* (mother) is not back."

Atama pulled the child and embraced her, saying,

"*Ma'ale* (mother) is fine and I am going to take you to her. By the way, my name is Atama; would you mind telling me yours?"

"Anu".

"Such a beautiful name, Anu."

"*Utamgbamala* Atama (thank you Aunty Atama).

"We will go to *Ma'ale* (mother), but first you must promise me that you will do as I say; okay?"

Anu nodded her head in affirmation.

"Do you want to go with your kitten?"

"Yes, please!"

"Okay. Quickly, let's go get your cape and we will go and meet *Ma'ale* (mother). She's waiting for us. Do not speak to anyone as we go; okay?"

"Okay, *Mala* Atama."

It was getting late and the clouds were heavy. Atama quickly took Anu by the hand while she clutched onto her kitten. They navigated their way through the city, following routes with less suspicion and piercing eyes.

Down the road, a soldier and a woman were openly making love by a corner on the street, moaning aloud from their lustful pleasures. Atama quickly shielded Anu's eyes with her hands from seeing the illicit act. They passed in a hurry.

Atama kept looking from left to right, lest any soldier appeared out of the blue and try to force her into any sexual affair.

As they approached the city gate, a soldier called out, "Hey, you skinny whore, come over here!" Atama turned her back and her first instinct was to dash off with Anu for their lives, but upon turning her back, she realized that the voice was not referring to her. There stood a slim damsel dressed seductively, revealing her luscious cleavages. Her makeup was heavily done, obviously out for the night business.

Relief washed over Atama as she realized the call was not for her. The soldier walked up to the damsel as Atama hurriedly rushed Anu out of sight, into the woods.

When they arrived, they met the anxious mother who was sitting restlessly by the cave entrance, anticipating their arrival.

"*Ma'ale!* (Mother!)" came a joyous scream, as Anu dashed into the open arms of her mother. Atama watched with teary eyes as mother and daughter reunite in a firm clinch. The woman let her tears flow without restraint. She sobbed uncontrollably like a baby herself.

Atama felt fulfilled. She could feel a sense of accomplishment that she had done something good for someone; she had brought joy and restored life to a dying mother and missing daughter. Oh, such unexplainable joy and pleasure flooded her heart. With that, she resolved to find Ruhu and tell him of all her successes and achievements.

Overwhelmed with joy, she found a new zeal and the determination to pursue her cause and achieve the mission.

That evening, they feasted on a wild caterpillar she found on her way to the city, and some wild fruits she picked on the way back. The small camp ate it excitedly by the fire, everyone at peace with their space.

After the meal, Anu was fast asleep with her kitten wrapped in her arms beside her mother.

The woman turned to Atama and said,

"*Utamgba* (Thank you) for everything *Mala* … (aunty…)."

"Atama is the name," Atama said, trying to help her out.

"*Male* Atama."

"I'm Malaika," the woman introduced herself.

"Princess Atama, we must not delay your mission. We are grateful and forever indebted to you for your kindness," Malaika expressed her gratitude.

"How did you know I'm the princess?" Atama was truly surprised, as she could not remember giving the woman such information about her identity.

The woman narrated,

“My husband, the baker that wouldn’t pledge his allegiance to Masisi, was killed and used as an example to whoever dared to resist the rulership of Masisi. He told me a story a few years ago, when we were courting, that there was a little girl in the palace of King Nyambe who would one day conquer and stop the rise of evil. She would have the powers to see and read minds, but she would also have close friends who would, in reality, be enemies. She must watch her back, else the enemy within would crash her before the arrival of the enemy without”.

“Hmm! So what makes you think I’m the princess?” Atama asked.

She smiled and continued,

“When I was on the verge of death that day, in my pain, I pleaded with Nyambe to save me and spare the life of my child. Then you showed up, having the ability to read my thoughts. I felt the presence of Nyambe and only a man consumed with the evil of Buwana’s powers will not smell the cleanness and purity emanating from your being. Even your breath has the aroma of life, hope and peace. So, I knew it must be the little princess that carried the veins of Nyambe."

Atama listened in silence and informed Malaika,

"I will go away for a while. You are strong enough to care for yourself and your daughter, Anu. The city is not safe for now, but you can stay here for a while until you can figure out what to do. I'll be gone before the first cockcrow tomorrow."

"Okay, I will like to give you a little gift."

Malaika loosened the edge of her wrapper and handed her three fine stones, saying,

"These were given to me by my husband on our wedding night. He told me they have life in them but I have never seen the life. Perhaps, they will breathe in the right hand or at the right time."

She continued,

"This stone," lifting the smallest one, "can grow into a rock. It's called the protector. This next one has the ability for speed, but it reduces its size to almost invisible and it keeps to time when sent on a mission. The last one keeps a secret. Now, I don't know how true this myth is. Maybe you will have to find out yourself."

"Whenever I teased that they were mere stones, my husband always say; you never know the powers within a thing until you activate them." She looked far away with a sad face as if missing her husband greatly.

"But I kept them because they were gifts and they were beautiful," She added.

"Well, I think they may come alive in the right hands," Malaika said, stretching out the stones to Princess Atama.

"Please accept them as a token of my appreciation."

Atama received the precious stones with gratitude, covered them with a piece of cloth and put them carefully in her backpack.

"*Utamgba* (thank you),"

Princess Atama said as she prepared a spot to lay her head for the night.

5

The journey to the mountains was a fierce one. Outside Malunga, there was a refreshing atmosphere and Ruhu enjoyed it with all pleasure. He could feel his mind being coordinated again, his powers surging up within him, as the thick dark cloud of Malunga that beclouded his focus gradually faded away. He knew this was not the time to try any form of escape for the sake of the princess and for the mission not to be aborted. He was willing to lay down his life for this cause, but he was in dilemma on how to save the scroll that contained the secrets to invoking Nyambe's signet ring.

With the clean atmosphere, Ruhu tried to contact Nyambe. Although it was a risky thing to do, he still had to try. He would be careful, but first, he must wait until it's dark.

"Tie the buffaloes to the trees. We shall camp here for the night," Masisi commanded.

The men did as they were told. There was a river down the slope where some of the soldiers decided to cool off while others made the campfire. A soldier kept an eye on Ruhu.

Ruhu was bound hands and feet. He was exhausted from the long walk and wished he could be let loose a bit, but they would not let him. They knew of his powers and would not risk it, or he would pull some form of mischief.

Masisi would not rest or get himself refreshed. He was too restless with power and the mission at hand to allow himself the leisure of rest. He took out calabash, candles, animal skin and the tooth of a leopard. He began to invoke dark powers for revelation, chanting incantations that would subdue any other power that might want to oppose him. Soon, all the soldiers fell into a deep sleep like logs of wood. The greenish smoke proceeding from the enchantment polluted the atmosphere, making Ruhu choke from the weight of the tormenting spirit. Snake-like creatures that had wings filled the air, swimming in all directions, beclouding the mind of Ruhu, and releasing the spirit of heaviness and slumber. They swam like bees. Ruhu kept scouting them away from forming a nest above his head, while Masisi watched to his pleasure and satisfaction.

These creatures formed a nest over their victims' bodies. Some perched on their heads, others on their chests, and some even went as far as to have intercourse with them. The soldiers cried out in pleasure, growing weaker and weaker, to the entertainment of Masisi. It was a disgusting scene for Ruhu, as he tried to guard his heart against being infiltrated while he tried to stay sane from the terrible buzz of those creatures over his head.

There was no way he could try any communication with Nyambe. The atmosphere was contaminated with evil and the distraction was too heavy to allow any form of concentration.

Seeing that he was going to be in this distress for a long time if he did not do anything to stop those creatures, he began to chant in an unknown tongue. The buzz of the creatures did not allow Masisi to notice or hear him chant. He kept at it and soon there were lightning and thunder in the sky. Before Masisi could realize what was happening, a heavy downpour of rain and hailstones, accompanied by lightning, struck the camp.

The soldiers woke up hysterically, running for shelter under the trees. The creatures vanished into vapours, and the buffalos scampered into the thick forest. Chaos took over the camp.

Thick darkness consumed the horizon. Masisi lightened up his eyes into a blue flame and began to grope in the dark, in search of his enchanting tools. The prisoner was soon forgotten as everyone dashed to save their dear lives.

It rained all through the night. By morning, the prisoner, Ruhu, was nowhere to be found. They searched around.

"Perhaps, the rain and hailstone have struck him dead," they thought, but there was no body, no footprint and no Ruhu.

"You fools!" cried Masisi, "How could you think he would be dead? Don't you know he was the cause of the chaos?"

In a rage, Masisi's eye turned into a flame of fire as he thundered,

"Find me that wizard and bring him here. He will pay dearly for this."

The search for Ruhu began.

***

Atama journeyed all day in the deep forest. When she was hungry, she searched for wild grapes, some cashew and guava. She ate as much as she needed, storing a handful in her backpack for the night.

Hours later, the sky was becoming dark. She found an oak tree where she retired for the night. Using her mind, she scouted the whole area to check out for any danger or evil lurking in the dark. Satisfied that her environment was clear, she laid her head to sleep.

The trees within the forest began to shake as something glowed in the dark.

The darkness thickened while the princess snored some more. The creeping sound kept coming closer and closer. Then three fierce-looking monkeys appeared before her with awful eyes and blood-stained mouths, obviously hunting for fresh blood.

Atama was in grave danger. She did not possess any weapon with which to defend herself, nor had she developed any skill for self-defence. There she was, fast asleep in the sight of inescapable danger.

The monkeys charged violently, in a bid to take out their prey. Suddenly, the smallest rock hidden in her bag came alive, jumped off the bag, turned into a giant rock and began to roll over the monkeys. The second rock, the rock of speed, flew out of the bag with great speed, caught up with the fleeing monkeys and knocked them off. The last rock, the rock of secrets, came out majestically, possessing magical hands and feet, got to the scene, pulled the three dead monkeys by their tails and brought them to the foot of the oak tree where Atama was sleeping and snoring. The rock dusted off its hands in satisfaction. Then, together, they all went back into the bag.

Atama turned to find a more comfortable position as she slept in great oblivion.

When morning came, she stretched and yawned as she came down from the oak tree, and beheld the wonder before her.

"How could this be? What happened last night?" She wondered.

How would she explain the death of three monkeys by her side?

"Could it be that Nyambe is really with me?" She wondered.

"This means no evil shall come near my dwelling. See how he fought my battles while I slept in safety. Truly,

Nyambe will keep his own in perfect peace, even in the face of danger."

"Thank you, King Nyambe. I shall remember that I'm not alone on this mission."

She took her belongings and walked past the dead monkeys in a newly found confidence of safety and protection.

***

The search for Ruhu continued for days. The soldiers were exhausted from the futile hunt.

Ruhu walked several miles to find his way to the great river. Crossing the river to the other side would take him to the place where the powers of Buwana were unreachable. There, the air was clear and had not been infiltrated by the evil powers of Buwana. He would be able to access his full powers and send arrows into the camp of Masisi to destroy his palace and disrupt his mission.

The long journey got him exhausted to his marrow. He was mostly hungry and his feet were full of sores. That greatly slowed his speed, as he also suffered great starvation, causing his vision to be blurred and making it difficult to have a bearing on the path he took. Soon, he lost track, as his body could not be sustained anymore. He slumped to the ground and fell into a deep sleep. On waking up, he found himself surrounded by Masisi's soldiers. They bound his feet and hands more firmly than they did previously.

The soldiers saddled him on their backs as they matched back to the camp, raining insults and curses on him for putting them in such hardship for days. They matched forward until they got to the camp and dumped him at the feet of the master, Masisi.

"You think you are wise, Ruhu?"

Masisi walked around him in mocking gestures, with his hands clocked behind.

"You are trying my patience, you wretch. I can see that you crave a pinch of my venom," Masisi threatened.

Ruhu said nothing, already too weak from the long walk and left with almost no energy in him.

"Answer me, you cunning godforsaken wizard!"

Masisi landed a heavy punch on Ruhu which threw him off balance and landed him harshly into the muddy earth.

"Take this fool and feed him. I need him alive for the mission. We'll climb the mountain top in three days," Masisi ordered the soldiers.

They dragged Ruhu away to a section of the camp to attend to his needs and wounds. He was fed with freshly hunted rabbit and wild guava. The soldiers were generous enough to hand him a portion of the wild honey they scooped from an oak tree they came across some days ago, with the carcasses of three monkeys at its foot.

Ruhu ate with much gratitude, feeling physically refreshed while he recuperated.

On the third day, the group decamped and set out for the mountains. They travelled for several miles until they came to the foot of Mape Mountain. The vegetation was thick and filled with wild monkeys. They did not bother themselves about that because the master was there and his powers were in charge at the moment.

It took a whole day to get to the mountaintop. There was no time for rest as Masisi ordered Ruhu to begin invoking the content of the scroll from the Stone Wall of Secrets.

Ruhu sat at a distance from the group with his legs crossed and his hands resting on his lap. He closed his eyes and then began to chant in a less humorous voice.

"zodowadiiiimunicepiiidodowadiiii, zodowadiiiiimunicepiiidodowadiii, zodowadiiiimunicepiiidodowadiii...," the chant was rising higher and higher and there was a reaction in the skies.

Deep darkness began to cover the horizon. From it, thick smoke began to rise. Then came a bright illumination, bringing forth written words from scrolls.

By now, Ruhu's eyes had turned white like that of a god. He was accessing secrets in the Stone Wall of Secrets and passing them into the animal skin Masisi had provided. For days, they were retrieving history through the mind of Ruhu and it began to drain the life out of him. It was a tedious task. If he continued for another day, he was surely going to lose his life. Blood had started flowing from his nostrils.

***

Atama had travelled for days and had almost lost hope when suddenly she stumbled upon the last location where the group had camped. Hope arose within her.

"But where exactly did they proceed to?"

She wondered, looking around her with no clue of the direction to take. She closed her eyes and tried to focus, perhaps she would see or hear a sound, but none came. An idea came to her mind. She reasoned that if they were once there, then she could trace their whereabouts from their footsteps.

Closing her eye, she tried to listen. She bent down, with her ears to the ground, and listened. There it was, tap, tap, tap, the sound of footsteps heading towards a direction behind her. Now she knew where to follow.

Paying attention to the sound of the footsteps, she realized that she could pick out footsteps belonging to every man. That of Ruhu was the loudest, beckoning her to hasten her steps. So, she did.

Taking off in a swift race, Atama could sense horror on the horizon. She tried to run faster, but the more she ran, the more distance she needed to cover. She tried focusing her mind on speed and boom!

The rock of speed in her backpack jumped out, swept her off her feet like a whirlwind, and in no time, she was at the foot of the mountain.

Quickly and quietly, she found a shed and hid. The cloud and lightning had covered the mountain.

Realizing she had not thought of a rescue plan, Atama rubbed and hit her head, scouting for the best move for the rescue mission.

Ruhu was on the last scroll that held the secret and was on the verge of death.

Atama closed her eyes and concentrated on Ruhu's mind. She appeared in his realm, took hold of the scroll and began to change the writings. She could see Ruhu's spirit gradually slipping out of his body.

"Ruhu, don't leave. Stay awake. You are the everlasting guardian of the Stone Wall of Secret. You have no equal and your power is matchless. Wake up. Do not allow evil to usurp your powers. Remember, evil will last only for a while but the powers of Nyambe will reign forever."

The words she spoke turned first into mist, vapour, and then droplets of water which Ruhu gulped down his throat. Immediately, it brought life into his body.

As soon as Ruhu's life was restored, the third rock, the rock of secret, appeared in a realm visible to only Ruhu and Atama. It opened up and swallowed the original scroll from Atama's hand, while the counterfeit was passed on to Masisi.

Nevertheless, Masisi was no fool. His instincts told him something was odd. Charging with wild anger, he stretched out his elongated hand to fetch Ruhu from the thick smoke, when suddenly a giant rock appeared before him, creating a barrier between them.

"Brace for attack!"

He commanded his troops. Drawing their swords, they charged towards the thick smoke.

On the other side of the rock, Ruhu had regained his strength and was running down the mountain towards Atama's hiding place. She met him halfway and they ran together.

"Look!" A soldier pointed towards their direction.

"The rebels are escaping!"

The soldiers shouted and so they charged after them. Masisi was in a rage. He began to invoke the dark powers to restrain them but the rock of speed appeared and went after him. He took to his heels but the rock caught up with him, knocking him down to his face. When the soldiers saw what happened, they were gripped with fear and retreated. They went over to their master to attend to him, while Atama and Ruhu escaped into the forest.

Princess Atama and Ruhu found a cave close to a fast-flowing river where they could spend the night. Exhaustion had taken the best part of their strength. Nevertheless, the joy of finding each another and escaping from the hands of the enemy superseded the pain and exhaustion they were feeling.

After washing their faces and taking a drink, too tired to hunt for meat, they shared some guava and wild grapes that Atama wrapped in a piece of cloth from her backpack.

Satisfied, they made the fire for the night.

As soon as they were refreshed, Atama wasted no time in telling Ruhu all about her ordeal and discoveries. She narrated the story of Malaika and her daughter, Anu, and the three dead monkeys she found after a long restful sleep. Ruhu was amused, watching his once stubborn and uncooperative girl find her true self in the face of chaos.

Atama told him about the three rocks and their powers. Jumping up, Atama ran to her backpack.

"That reminds me, the rocks," reaching through her backpack, "I think I've lost them," she cried.

"Are you sure about that? Look again," Ruhu urged.

"No one can lose the rocks. They are faithful and stay true to their owner. No matter where they go, they will surely return." Ruhu assured her.

"Really?"

And there they were, all three of them wrapped in the piece of animal skin that Malaika had placed them.

"Indeed, they are truly faithful," smiled Atama as she covered them, putting them carefully into her backpack.

"Let us take some rest. Tomorrow, we shall cross the river. I must show you something. A greater enemy lies ahead of our mission. The enemy within must be subdued ahead of time," Ruhu told the princess.

6

Something smelled good. The aroma of burnt animal skin and fresh meat filled the atmosphere.

Atama turned and tossed in her sleep. Finally, consumed by the aroma, she succumbed to the temptation and bid sleep goodbye.

Her instincts were right. Ruhu was making a delicious breakfast of freshly hunted wild rabbits. He was roasting the meat on a stake and whistling something under his breath. He seemed calm and relaxed, and quite focused on what he was doing, or could it be he had something else on his mind?

"Good morning, Ruhu," Atama greeted.

"Ah! I see you are awake. Good morning, my dear. Did you sleep well last night?" Ruhu asked.

"Oh, I did! It felt like I hadn't had a good sleep in a long while. Did you know I almost didn't know I was alive? I indeed had a sound sleep," she said.

"Good to hear that. You know when the heart is at peace, even in the face of turbulence and chaos, it often reflects in the sleep."

"What about you? Did you sleep well?" Atama asked.

"Or perhaps you had dreams of freshly roasted rabbit and decided to cut down your sleep, just for the taste of it?"

"Hahaha!" Ruhu laughed humorously.

"Well, I indeed had a peaceful night's rest, especially with the serene atmosphere; but most importantly because I know that you are safe and hope lies ahead of us."

"And talking about the rabbit, I thought it would be a good meal for our bodies. Having gone through the fires and coming out alive, we deserve a nice treat."

"Hmmm!" Looking suspiciously at Ruhu, as if he had more to say.

"Okay, okay, I know." Ruhu smiled, looking Atama in the eye with all seriousness.

"I just wanted to make you happy. It's my way of saying I'm proud of you. I'm proud of the woman you are becoming. You could have stayed in Malunga and remained indifferent and rebellious, but you came after me, knowing you have little skill for battle. It means a lot to me."

"This is my way of saying thank you."

He smiled a little and winked at her, as he passed her a portion of the meat.

She started to smile, then burst out laughing. They both started laughing as she received the meat from him.

It was lovely to feast on a delicious meal while they chatted and laughed in the peace of the moment.

It felt safe and normal again. It felt beautiful, just like in the good days when Atama and Makundu would visit Ruhu in the Stone Wall of Secrets. He would tell them stories, mostly of the future; stories of light being stored in glasses, like bottles, made to illuminate at night without burning lambs. He would tell them stories of giant objects having four legs like the buffalo, transporting people with the speed of the rushing river, and stories of objects like birds flying up in the sky with people inside.

Those stories fascinated them. They could not believe that it was possible, yet Ruhu painted pictures of those objects in their minds, making them look real.

They loved playing and listening to Ruhu.

Above telling them those stories, he also listened to the imaginations of their hearts. He would listen to all their childish chants and stories, and he would laugh and tickle them.

Atama remembered pieces of those lovely days and felt like she was living in such a moment.

They finished their breakfast in silence and the peace of each other's space.

"Thank you, Ruhu for the meal. It was delicious."

"You're welcome, my dear."

The two decamped and headed for the great river.

They walked for about five miles before coming across the River Galana-Sabaki. The tides were high due to the high amount of rainfall.

It was her first time seeing the great river, although Ruhu had told them stories about it. Standing before it sent chills into her heart.

River Galana-Sabaki was truly beautiful. It rose like a whirlwind, flowing strongly in a series of rapids, turbid and yellow in colour. The waterfalls were incredibly beautiful. She could spot hippopotamus swimming lazily in the river, and the crocodiles gathered at the bank as if they were the lords of the river.

Ruhu closed his eyes and drank in the cool breeze. It was refreshing and it carried an ounce of hope along with it.

"We must move forward," Ruhu said, turning to Atama.

"But how do we cross the river?" Atama expressed her worry.

"The crocodiles," Ruhu responded.

Ruhu beckoned on them. The crocodiles swamped towards their direction.

When they were within sight, Atama noticed they were not the usual crocodiles. These had transparent bodies with a crystal appearance. One could see through them.

It was truly amazing.

They had crystal blue fluid flowing in a streamlined manner through their bodies. Their teeth were silver. Their faces had quite an intriguing shape with the mouths curving as if to a smile, and the fierce-looking eyes leaving an impression that they could see deep into one's soul.

"They are immortal," Ruhu said.

"Really?" Atama asked, very curious.

"Yes, and they can see deep into the soul of a man. They will only transport a person with a clean heart such as theirs. A dirty heart sends a threat signal to them and that means to attack. That is why the powers of Buwana cannot get across the river to the other side. The crocodile will attack it fiercely."

"I see!"

"As you can see through them, so also can they see through you. Nothing is hidden and nothing is evil within them."

Fascinated by these creatures, Atama moved closer to have a better view. The crocodiles also focused their piercing eyes on her, scanning through her soul. They did the same with Ruhu before allowing them access to their backs. They navigated through the great river for hours before getting to the other side of it.

***

It had been days since they crossed River Galana-Sabaki to Amani, a land of peace and tranquillity.

The landscape was beautiful, housing lush rolling hills, vast waterfalls, lakes, and green savannah vegetation. The wildlife was beautiful.

Atama sat on a hill and watched the leopards, buffalos, antelopes, elephants, lions and other animals race and play with their kids peacefully.

There were no prey and hunters. The animals harmoniously enjoyed their existence.

Ruhu and Atama explored the land, taking a few days to rest and drink its beauty. They lay on the grass on the hills, basking in the fresh morning sun. They visited the waterfalls and Atama took advantage of the serenity to take a bath. They ate fresh mangoes, sweet melons and pawpaw. They were truly refreshed.

"Training begins tomorrow," Ruhu called out to Atama who was enjoying a ride on an elephant's back.

"What training? Can't we just enjoy the peace and beauty of Amani?" She replied as the wind carried her voice away.

Ruhu watched her spread her hands, lifting her head to the rays of the sun. She was swimming in the pleasure, but they must continue with the mission ahead. She must be trained in the use of weapons and the skills of war.

In the morning, Atama opened her eyes to different weapons laid before her. While she was scavenging the land and its beauty, Ruhu was scouting for bones and jaws of dead animals, making weapons out of them. The jaw of the lion, the legs of a giraffe, and the skulls and skeletons of several dead animals were shaped into amazing weapons.

"Pick a choice of weapon," he urged her.

She picked a long spear.

"You have chosen well. I will teach you its use."

"Now brace up," Ruhu commanded in a tone of absolute seriousness, putting all pleasure and laxity aside.

"Rule number one, 'never underestimate the enemy'. He is smart, skilled, cunning, determined and resilient."

"Rule number two, 'never be afraid of the enemy.' He will come like a mighty wind, hurling insults and curses like a tornado. He will appear in vicious apparel, possessing devastating weapons. This is to plant an image of defeat in your mind even before the battle begins. He will use demeaning words, a fierce appearance, and a show of his weapon to attack your mind. Don't fall for it," Ruhu warned.

Atama listened attentively.

"Remember, your victory and the defeat of the enemy starts from your mind. Before you engage, always remember who you are, the heir of Nyambe. His blood runs through your veins. So, you are more than a conqueror."

Ruhu took the spear from Atama, positioning himself for a strike. He turned slowly with the skill of 'striking and focus', then struck into the air.

Atama watched with keen interest.

He placed the spear in her hands, positioned it, and carefully they practised the rule of 'striking and focus.'

For weeks, they practised different skills. They practised focus, speed, strength, resilience, and the use of instincts.

Atama was stretched vigorously to the point of exhaustion. They ran along with the cheetah. They tested their strength with the lion and mastered the act of targeting and throwing the spear from a distance to meet a target on a marked tree.

Atama's muscles grew. She gained stamina and resilience. Ruhu was pleased with her determination to learn and conquer.

"Every preparation must be tested," Ruhu said to her, "We'll set out for Mape Mountain tomorrow. There, we shall test your strength and skill as you face the fierce and carnivorous Mape monkeys."

The sun had set on the mountains. They had had a fulfilled day.

"It's a good time to rest and refresh yourself for what lies ahead," Ruhu urged Atama to retire early for the night.

The night grew darker than usual. The thick vegetation of the Mape Mountains hurled thick sheds of evil and danger filled the atmosphere. The trees were dancing, while thunder strikes and lightning were ravening. The mountain looked like it was in a quake.

Two monkeys with eyes burning like flames of fire appeared out of the dark, with carnivorous teeth, ready for attack. Atama was scared. Her first instinct was to run. She threw away her spear and took off, running deeper into the mountain. The monkeys angrily went after their prey with firm determination to devour.

Atama ran for her dear life, not knowing where she was headed nor the danger that lay ahead. Her mission right then was to save her life, nothing else.

She found an oak tree and hid there.

She could hear their movement, jumping from one tree to another, scavenging for her. Each heartbeat drew them closer. Fear gripped her soul.

"Oh, I'm going to die! Where is Ruhu? Where is Nyambe? Oh no, I'm finished!" She screamed.

Finally, the monkeys got to the oak tree and began to shake it violently.

Atama ran out of the tree but not so fast, for she was restrained by one of the monkeys.

"Please, don't kill me. Please, please, please," she pleaded.

Now she was caught in between the two monkeys.

They kept getting closer, with the sole aim of devouring their prey.

Atama looked left and right, but no escape route surfaced.

"Please, please, please," she pleaded again.

This time, the monkeys were determined to crush her. They charged towards her.

"Help! Ruhu, help!!" She screamed with her eyes closed.

Immediately, a flash of lightning appeared like a shield around her, while the two monkeys were caught in a web.

When she opened her eyes, gasping for breath, Ruhu was standing right in front of her.

"It's okay, dear one," he reassured her.

She noticed that the night was just settling in, and they were still in Amani.

"Was it a dream?" She wondered.

Turning to Ruhu.

"I had a dream, it felt so real. I was at Mape Mountain fighting two carnivorous monkeys. They almost killed me, but…"

"It wasn't a dream," Ruhu interrupted her, "I only simulated the test. I was there all along, watching and waiting for you to call for help".

"Really?" Atama's face was sad "So, I failed the test I guess."

"No, you didn't, although you fell for the enemy's tricks. You allowed fear to consume you. You threw away your weapon and believed the lie that you were going to die."

"But would I have been killed?"

"Yes, if you hadn't called out for help."

"No matter the situation or the fierceness in battle, call out for help. You know we play by the rules, and I cannot indulge in the fight unless you ask for my help. That way, I get the legal ground to step in," Ruhu enlightened her.

"Hmm! I see."

Atama took a deep breath, taking in all corrections with a better and deeper understanding.

"Now, get some rest. Tomorrow, we head out to Mape Mountain. Remember, the monkeys will be more than two in Mape. Put your training to use. Lastly, call for help when you need it."

"Good night, dear one."

"Good night, Ruhu."

At dawn, they set out on their journey. They crossed the great River Galana-Sabaki on the crocodile's back. They travelled for another three days before getting to Mape Mountain.

The sun was setting when they got there. So, they decided to camp for the night and begin climbing the next day.

At dawn, Ruhu woke Atama up, saying,

"It's time. Get your weapon."

Atama arose with a determination to win the battle this time.

They travelled for two hours before they started sensing the monkeys locking between the trees and making vicious sounds in preparation to attack.

Slowly they matched forward, Atama holding her spear and positioning herself for attack or defence. Ruhu was holding a lion's jaw. Slowly they approached.

Suddenly, an ugly monkey surfaced before them. Atama targeted, focused and sent her spear flying into the brain of the monkey. It jumped hysterically before dropping dead. Atama was filled with excitement, turning to ask Ruhu if he saw that, but Ruhu was nowhere to be found. He had vanished.

She was confused.

"Ruhu, where are you?" She called out.

"Okay, is this a joke?"

Atama shook her head. "Could this be another test?" She wondered, but not for long, as she noticed fifteen monkeys heading towards her direction with wild eyes and blood-stained mouths.

Fear gripped her. She looked to her left, there lay her spear right in the brain of the monkey she had just killed. She was at a fix; no spear and no Ruhu.

"Run, run," her instinct demanded. So, she took off, running with all her strength and might, and the monkeys came after her.

She tried to remember what Ruhu had taught her but to no avail.

"Ruhu, where are you? Please help me!" She cried bitterly.

"Do not be afraid. Remember, you are the heir to the great Nyambe's throne. You must face your fears and fight," came the voice of Ruhu in her mind.

With that, she halted, turned around, and right beside her was Ruhu's lion jaw, lying on the ground. She picked it up. With great strength and with a skill she did not know she possessed, she began to smash the brains and cut the limbs of her attackers.

She uprooted necks and sliced the monkeys into two. She was fighting vigorously.

A monkey jumped unto her head. She turned and struggled to take it off but it held on, scratching her hair and looking for the best part to plant a bite. She struggled tirelessly, but the monkey seemed to be overpowering her.

With firm resolve, she found the monkey's mouth, reached out and ripped it apart with her bare hands.

Only two monkeys were left, and as soon as they witnessed the terror, they fled, jumping hysterically from tree to tree and into the woods.

She retrieved her spear, drawing it off the carcass of the monkey. Holding unto the lion's jaw in the other hand, she marched on. This time, she was braced up and ready for more battles.

She marched on, going deeper into the woods and scavenging for more prey.

Suddenly, the mountain seemed quiet and no attack was hauled at her. The monkeys seemed to have left her alone.

As she approached, two monkeys saw her and ran for their lives.

"Better run," she thought to herself.

Down the slope, she saw a baby monkey trapped in a tree. Upon seeing her, it struggled to free itself to flee, but to no avail. The baby monkey cried and struggled.

Atama's heart went out in compassion for the monkey. It looked at her pitifully, as if pleading to be spared.

"Look, I'm not going to attack you unless you attack me. Relax, let me free your limbs."

When the monkey tried to resist her touch out of fear, she reassures it.

"Relax, I'm not going to hurt you. I'm not the enemy."

As soon as she freed its limbs, three monkeys hanging on the tree above them bent down and tied her hands and legs, lifting her. It was a trap.

The little monkey she helped stuck out its tongue, wiggling it with its hands to its ears. It made mockery gestures, danced and shook its butt at her before dashing off to its mama sitting upon a tree.

"Do not underestimate the enemy; he is smart and cunning," she remembered Ruhu's lessons.

She was tied with her feet and her hands were spread across the tree's branches with no form of defence or escape route. Feeling powerless, defeat gradually started to settle in.

"Always ask for help when you need one," she heard the voice of Ruhu.

Immediately, Atama called out, "Help! Help!"

Suddenly, the three rocks flew out of her backpack. The giant rock stood as a shield before Atama, while the rock of speed began to knock them on the heads, killing them without mercy. The rock of secret, using its hands and feet, climbed upon the giant rock and began to lose her.

She was free and grateful for the rescue.

"Come over here; there is fresh water to drink," Ruhu's voice called out.

"Ruhu!"

Atama was excited, "where did you go to? I couldn't find you."

"Congratulations." Ruhu smiled at her.

"You passed the test. I was there all along, only that I was invisible, for the teacher doesn't distract during a test."

He was wearing a big smile. He handed her water from animal skin.

"You have made me proud," Ruhu said boastfully.

She took the water.

"Thank you," she said as she drank and returned the jar to Ruhu.

Ruhu took out a red headband and placed it on her head.

"This is a gift for the battle you have won."

Atama knelt and he tied a blue rope on her right upper arm, saying, "This is for courage."

Finally, he took a bottle containing the blood of a lioness, dipped his thumb in it, then marked her forehead with it, laying his hands upon her head.

"The mark of the lion is a mark of victory. You are undefeatable. I now pronounce you a warrior."

"Arise, Warrior Atama, the heir to the great King Nyambe." The clouds stroke with thunder as the ritual was completed.

Atama arose with a spear in her right hand and a lion's jaw in the left, bearing the mark of a lion and a band for courage and victory.

"We shall build an army called 'The Resistance.' The battle is fierce and the enemy is getting set. I shall return to Amani. You, however, will go back to Malunga and recruit men, women and children who have not pledged allegiance to the powers of Buwana. Bring them over to Amani where I shall train them in the skill of a soldier."

"Bring in only those who have not bowed. We shall build an army for the battle ahead."

With that, Ruhu returned to Amani, while Atama set out for Malunga.

7

It had been a month since Masisi and his team came back from the Mape Mountains, bastardly defeated. He raged and took out his frustration on anyone who crossed his path, starting with Zuchi.

Masisi, upon his return, had demanded that the princess be brought before him, and of course, Zuchi was brought to him.

"Princess Zuchi, you will pay for Ruhu's escape, and for sending your maid after us. She helped him escape, and now our mission has failed."

"Guards, take this witch away," he commanded.

Zuchi was arrested and thrown into the dungeon with the young guard to watch over her.

"What could have happened to Ruhu and Princess Atama?" Zuchi wondered.

"Are they still alive? Will they come for me? What will become of me if they don't return? I need to think of a plan as fast as I can, or else I will rot here for nothing," she thought to herself.

Days passed but there was still no sign of Princess Atama or Ruhu. Zuchi became scared and worried about her fate. She lost her appetite and ate nothing for days. The young guard watching over her feared she had died one morning when he called her and did not hear her response.

"Princess Zuchi, are you still there? Can you hear me?" He called out.

"Are you okay?" he tried again but there was still no response. He opened the cell and turned her over as she was sleeping huddled up in a corner.

"Oh no, you are shivering," he noticed. He touched her forehead, it was burning with a fever.

"You need to be treated; else master shall lose you too."

"Water, I want water please," she whispered weakly.

The young guard reached out for a water jar nearby and gave her a drink. She sipped the water and then closed her eyes.

"Wake up, wake up," he shook her, afraid she had suddenly died.

She mustered up the energy to whisper "thank you," simply to reassure him that she was still alive.

He got a wet cloth and placed it on her forehead to reduce her body temperature. Then he brought some rabbit stew from the kitchen and quickly fed her before the other guards would see them.

The next day, he brought some herbs for her to take, a mixture of ginger, garlic, moringa and green leaf. She took it for several days until the fever broke and she felt better.

One night, Zuchi cried out in her sleep, "Nyambe, where are you? Princess Atama, where are you? I can't take this anymore. Come and deliver me from the hands of Masisi, before he feeds my flesh to the crocodiles. I don't want to be the princess anymore," she lamented.

"The burden is too much," she cried and said quite a lot in her sleep.

The guard overheard her and was confused. He wondered if she was dreaming or fully awake. He decided to confront her in the morning.

The next day, Masisi sent the young guard on an errand and had to replace him with another soldier. When Zuchi woke up, she was disappointed to see that he was gone.

She had woken up feeling a lot better, as the fever was gone. However, something else was troubling her. The thought of her fate overwhelmed her.

"What if Ruhu and Princess Atama do not return? What if Masisi decides to execute me? The mission will still go on and, since I am dispensable, I will be forgotten. I'm just a servant. What does Nyambe or Atama care about my life? And if they did care, then why are they not here now to save me?"

Zuchi remained truly troubled, thinking of the next step to take to save her life.

***

Life, meanwhile, was becoming unbearable for the people of Malunga. Masisi kept them preoccupied with all sorts of activities and physical labour, which they had come to accept as their fate.

The powers of Buwana were used to build tall buildings, machines that milled grains, and others that tilled the ground and harvested the crops. The people of Malunga were fascinated by the inventions and wondered at the powers of Buwana.

Still, they worked so hard and were forced to pay heavy taxes. However, they enjoyed the moonlight events where half-dressed women danced and showed off their buttocks, while the men drank into stupor through the night.

Masisi made sure they were preoccupied so that the thought or strength for a revolution will be impossible to muster, and his influence and powers would be accepted as the norm in Malunga.

Over time, the people gradually began to lose hope in Nyambe, and the thought of his powers rescuing them from the powers of Buwana became a myth for many.

They were discouraged and hopeless. So, eventually, they decided to flow with the new norm and bowed to Buwana. After all, there were lots of benefits they did not have or enjoy during the reign of Nyambe that they now enjoyed, they thought. So, they decided they would manage the new norm.

"I see you are looking better today," Zuchi turned as she heard the familiar voice, days later.

"Oh, you are back! I never got the chance to say thank you," she said as she stood up from the bed of straw and straightened her clothes.

"Thank you for nursing me back to health, even though I am your prisoner," Zuchi thanked the young guard.

"Masisi's prisoner, not mine," he corrected her before adding, "He needs you alive or my head will be on the stake down the road."

"I suppose you didn't nurse me to save your head, did you?"

"Well, that's one of the reasons, but not totally. I also nursed you because I'm human. I'm not a beast. Although I serve and have pledged my allegiance to the powers of Buwana, I do not agree with Masisi's methods of leadership. I have a mind of my own. My mother used to say she didn't know if I was a blessing or a curse to her," he shrugged.

"She still believes in the return of Nyambe, even though my father died from cholera after she had called on Nyambe to save him but he didn't."

The young guard continued, "My parents were fools. That I can tell you, but I'm not one."

"I see!" Zuchi responded.

"So, should I call you Zuchi or Princess Zuchi? I'm curious you know."

Zuchi looked at him, confused.

"Are you going to still keep your secret from me? I heard you in your sleep the other day lamenting and calling on Nyambe to come to save you. You are not the princess," the young guard declared confidently.

Zuchi was dumbfounded.

"Em! Em! Em!" she stammered.

"No need for that, Zuchi. I shall keep your little secret for now.

The guard had a brief pause. Then he continued,

"By the way, my name is Kiyambo, the son of late Natutu, the Zebra hunter." He winked at her, before heading to get fresh water from the kitchen, leaving Zuchi in silence.

Zuchi tried to think of an escape route for her dear life but to no avail. The temptation to give up was overwhelming. Finally, she resolved to save her life in whichever way she could.

***

Masisi had spent a lot of time in his dark room, mixing different algae and consulting the powers of Buwana for the next move in defeating Nyambe. "Deceit. Yes, that's the answer," he had a cocky smile on his face.

"I know exactly what to do," he boasted.

The next morning, Kiyambo, the young guard, was sent to fetch Zuchi from the dungeon. Zuchi knelt before Masisi with her hands tied.

"Your father Nyambe is weak and powerless. If not, why is he hiding? Why hasn't he come to rescue you from my hands? Now, I will show you what I have reduced him to."

Zuchi looked wide-eyed, still acting the role of the princess. Masisi opened a large pot filled with water. He stirred it, adding different colours of powder into it and chanting incantations until an image showed up. It was an image of Nyambe down on his knees, pleading for his life. Masisi was standing right in front of him with his crown.

Nyambe was crownless, looking tired and battered. There was mud on his face and defeat all around him. He stretched out his hands as if to reach for the crown, but Masisi struck him with his horn. The image of Nyambe falling to the ground struck Zuchi's heart. The tears flowed effortlessly. She was heartbroken to see the hope of Malunga in shame and defeat.

"Wipe your tears away, princess," Masisi said and, ending the vision, turned to make her an offer.

"You have seen for yourself the defeat of your father. Thanks to the powers of Buwana."

He came close to her, walked around her and said,

"Since I have defeated your father, I thought of killing you. But on second thought, there's no need for that, after all, I need a wife. So, I will make you an offer; marry me, and together we shall build a vast kingdom that will reach the heavens. Malunga will be ours forever. It's your only chance of survival unless you want to go join your father and brother in the grave."

Masisi put his hands into a black giant pot and pulled out a six-inch cobra. He brought it close to her neck to intimidate her and scare her into being on his side.

Zuchi wiped away her tears and thought to herself.

"This is an opportunity for me. I have nothing to lose if I accept the offer, after all, Nyambe has been defeated, and Ruhu and Princess Atama are nowhere to be found. I will take my chances. This is an opportunity to save my life and to become a queen."

Zuchi's plan initially was to throw herself at the mercy of Masisi by revealing her true identity, to save her life. However, with this deal of becoming a queen, she decided to keep the truth to herself and took the offer without a second thought.

Masisi brought the snake close to her neck so she could feel the flick of the snake's tongue. She shivered in fear.

"I shall do as you have said," she responded, acting as though she had succumbed based on fear, while her heart skipped with joy.

On hearing that, Masisi gave a cocky smile.

"My plan is working," he thought to himself, rejoicing in his heart.

Soon, the wedding was announced and preparations began. A few days before the wedding, Kiyambo met Zuchi by the balcony, facing east of the kingdom.

"I see you now have an escape route. Soon, a mere servant will become queen. What an ordeal!"

"What do you want?"

Zuchi asked as she looked sideways, hoping that no one was within earshot to overhear their conversation.

"You will be my mistress," Kiyambo told her.

"Kiyambo, you are crazy. Have you lost your mind? How can you be such a pervert?" Zuchi asked as she could not control her temper.

"Pervert? Everyone in Malunga is now a pervert and so are you, as long as you pledge your allegiance to the powers of Buwana. Now listen to me, you will do exactly as I say or I shall take your little secret to Masisi, and by noon, instead of a crown sitting upon your head, it will rather be on one of the stakes down the road."

Kiyambo laughed out loud, winked at Zuchi and quickly added before turning to leave, "I will do you good; don't worry."

With that, he whistled joyfully, as he walked back to his duty post by the rear entrance to the kingdom.

8

At last, Atama reached the cave after several days of trekking. She longed for a drink but first, she wanted to find Malaika and her daughter Anu, and ensure they are still alive and in good health, before continuing on her journey.

She got to the cave but noticed the place looked deserted. She moved closer to get a better view.

"Ma'ale, Ma'ale Malaika, Anu!"

She called out but there was no response. She began to panic.

"What if the soldiers found them? Oh my God! What if they died of hunger or a wild animal feasted on them?"

The thought of a wild forest goat or monkey licking Anu's brain sent chills down her spine. She quickly diverted the negative thought from her imagination, forcing her mind to stay positive.

Atama closed her eyes. She tried to see and hear with her inner eyes and ears. Soon, she saw little footprints and a bigger one belonging to an adult heading towards a direction. She could hear their voices singing something about the powers of Buwana under their feet and the powers of Nyambe inside their hearts. The voices were theirs.

Those were Anu and Malaika, her mother. Joy filled Atama's heart as she followed the voices into very thick vegetation. The place looked hidden; no one would ever imagine that it was a hideout.

When she got to the hideout, she noticed it was a clean and beautiful environment that turned into a home. It had a small vegetable garden to the left. The drying rope was dangling carelessly to the ends of a pole. There was a dirty rubber baby with a missing arm lying on the floor. It looked abandoned.

Atama could smell the aroma of a fresh rabbit. She was still taking in her environment when the thatched room door flung open.

"Princess Atama!" A wide-eyed Anu screamed, before dashing into the arms of Atama. Atama gripped her with so much joy and relief.

"Princess Atama," came Malaika behind her daughter, hugging Atama with so much excitement.

"Thank you great Nyambe, for bringing her here to us." Malaika was full of joy.

"How have you been?" She asked.

"You look well and strong," she added, looking at the muscles on Atama's arm, the blue arm band and the red headband on her forehead.

"You are now a warrior," Malaika said with understanding, looking Atama in the eye, not hiding how proud she was of her.

"Please, come in and rest. We have a lot to catch up on, but first, you need to rest and have a drink while I serve you fresh rabbit stew with wrapped starch."

"Thank you," Atama said gratefully as they entered the little thatched-roof house.

"You all don't look bad yourselves," Atama commented as they sat to enjoy their meal.

"We are more well and alive now that you are here," Malaika added. "We have enjoyed our peace and space ever since, although a lot has happened since you left a year ago. Before I tell you our story, please tell us what has happened to you; we are curious."

Atama smiled lovingly.

"Well, I can tell you that I went through the process of what I shall call 'the making of a warrior' from a foolish, self-centred and weak girl."

"Ah!"

They all laughed humorously.

"But in all seriousness, I went through the funnel of affliction to produce these strong muscles and to earn the mark of the lion on my forehead."

Malaika nodded with deep understanding.

Atama went on to narrate the events, starting from the wonder of the three rocks Malaika gave her as gifts, to the three dead monkeys on a night she slept like a baby with no military skills or weapon to defend herself, yet the spirit of Nyambe protected her from the carnivorous monkeys that would have feasted on her. She narrated the defeat of Masisi on Mape Mountain. She also told them about the beauty of the great River Galana-Sabaki, the land of Amani, the ordeal at the Mape Mountain and her present mission which was to recruit the army of the resistance."

Malaika listened with much interest and understanding. Anu enjoyed the story about the land of Amani.

"Can we also visit Amani and ride on an elephant's back?" Anu turned to ask Atama.

"Why not, little one? We can all do and become anything we want to be in this universe," Atama responded with a smile.

With joy, she turned to her mother and asked, "Mama, can we go to Amani tomorrow?"

The adults burst into laughter.

"Of course, not tomorrow but soon. We shall be the first to enlist in the army of the resistance," she said, answering her daughter while looking Atama in the eye.

"If you will have us, we would like to enlist in the army."

Atama was dumbfounded, full of joy, with teary eyes, lacking words to express her gratitude.

"When you return, I will take you somewhere," Malaika said to Atama, "and please be careful out there; do not let your guard down. Be careful because the enemy within is far greater than the enemy without."

"What do you mean by that?" Atama asked, as she also remembered Ruhu had made mention of that sometime back, but she had forgotten to ask him about this enemy.

"Just be careful, princess. Remember to be as wise as a serpent and beware of the teeth that bite the finger."

With that, they bid each other farewell. Atama promised to return as soon as she could. However, she had to visit Zuchi. They had a lot to talk about and strategize about their next move.

***

Atama disguised herself as a seamstress from another region, seeking new customers for her business. She waited in an inn until nightfall when she sneaked into the palace and found her way to Zuchi's chambers.

Zuchi was going about her business in the lower chambers with Kiyambo, her secret partner. She had just sneaked back to her chambers, certain that no one had seen or followed her. She closed the door quietly, put on the lamp and took off her cape. She sighed and was about to sit on the bed when a voice came from the shadow behind her.

"I see you, my princess."

Zuchi jumped up in fear, as she turned to face Princess Atama. She lifted the lamp to confirm it was truly Atama. They stared at each other for a while before Atama stepped forward and pulled her into a tight embrace.

"Oh, how I have missed you, my friend!" Atama said.

"It's so good to see you after all this while. How have you been holding up? How did you survive this place? I hope the demon-possessed Masisi did not lay his hands on you."

"I'm fine, as you can see. Please, forget about me. Let's sit," she pulled her to the bed.

"Tell me all that has happened to you. I am super curious and relieved at the same time. I thought something bad had happened to you. I thought you weren't coming back for me. Thank goodness you are here. Where is Ruhu? How is he? How did you escape and how did you manage to survive in the forest?"

"Calm down, Zuchi. Take it easy. We have the whole night to catch up and I will tell you everything."

Atama began to narrate the story, starting with how she met Malaika and the three secret stones and their magical powers. She went on to tell her about the great River Galana-Sabaki, about the land of Amani and its beauty, its vegetation, the peaceful wild animals and the waterfalls. Zuchi listened with great interest, paying apt attention to every detail.

"Now, I'm on a mission," Atama continued.

"I must recruit the remnant that hasn't bowed to the powers of Buwana or pledged allegiance to Masisi. They will be called the "army of the resistance." They shall meet with Ruhu at Amani for the training. We must get ready for the battle ahead. I don't have much time. I must go through the city to scout for them. Then we shall leave together. To avoid much suspicion, wait until nightfall, then meet me by the town's abattoir. Do you understand?" Zuchi nodded her head in agreement.

"I must start my work this night," Atama stood up to take her to leave.

"So soon?" Zuchi objected, "Please, at least spend the night with me. It's dark outside and the city is dangerous at night."

"No, Zuchi. I must go now," she laid her hand upon hers and was about to leave when she noticed the golden ring shaped into a skull on her finger. Atama froze for a while.

"Zuchi, why do you have Masisi's ring on your finger?" Zuchi quickly withdrew her finger, hiding it behind her.

"Oh no!" cried Atama.

"You are Masisi's bride? How could you marry the enemy? How could you sell your soul for temporal glory? You were supposed to pledge your allegiance to Nyambe with your life; you were supposed to serve."

"Excuse me, princess, hold it please!" Zuchi snapped at Atama.

"You and Ruhu abandoned me to the mercy of Masisi. He was angry about his defeat at Mape Mountain and threatened to kill me, but somehow, he was able to gain access to the whereabouts of Nyambe and there, he defeated him himself. I saw it with my own eyes. The crown was taken away from Nyambe, while he lay helpless in the dust of the earth. I had no choice. Masisi still thinks I'm the princess. So, he offered me an option to be his queen or be struck dead by his poisonous snake; and trust me, I know better than to reject the offer."

"Really? Zuchi, you fell for the deceit that the great Nyambe is defeated and dead? How does that sound to you? Your heart was already weak even before the offer. So, don't you dare tell me you had no choice."

"And don't you dare stand there and judge me!" Zuchi flared back. "I did what I had to do to stay alive. After all, you and Ruhu had abandoned me and had been gone for over a year now," Zuchi was agitated.

"Watch your tongue with me, girl!" Atama retorted.

"And mind your attitude before me, for I'm the queen in this kingdom," Zuchi stormed back.

"Ah! I see."

Atama was dumbfounded. At that moment, she felt more stupid than betrayed that she had told the whole truth to the enemy. How foolish of her! Atama turned and walked out of the room quietly with a raging heart on fire.

By midnight she found her way back to Malaika's little home, in need of refuge and a shoulder to lean and cry on.

Malaika opened the door quietly. She put on the lamp, made something hot for the night and they sat outside on a tree trunk sipping their drink, while Atama poured out her heart.

"I met the enemy within and she bit my fingers badly; but not until I had let my guard down and was foolish enough to reveal the whole plan and mission to recruit the army of the resistance. Right now, I feel like I have already failed the mission even before I begin. It's like going straight to the enemy to reveal the exact place he should shoot you in the leg."

A tear escaped Atama's eye. Zuchi was the last person she had ever thought would betray her. She felt sad and regret flooded her mind.

"If only I had kept my guard up, if only I had used my powers to read the state of her mind, I would have had a clue that she now belongs to the devil. How foolish was I to not have been as wise as the serpent!" She lamented while Malaika tried to comfort her.

"I felt there was something bad ahead but didn't know what it was," Malaika said.

"Anyway, I shall take you somewhere in the morning, perhaps it will bring you fresh hope."

"Where is that?"

"Don't worry." Rising, Malaika said, "Let's go get some sleep, and by daybreak, I will take you there."

9

They walked for hours into the bush. It would have been a short distance from Malaika's house through the small river, but because it was the rainy season; the river was full and the tides were high. So, they had to walk a long distance. Finally, they arrived at a cave entrance. Malaika clapped her hands three times. A young man came forth from a tree trunk behind them. He was the guard on duty, camouflaged in green leaves.

"Greetings, Malaika, and who is this?" The guard asked curiously with an unfriendly tone.

"May I speak with Zatanya, please?" Malaika pleaded.

"Why? Not with a stranger, you know," the guard insisted.

"She is not an ordinary stranger; she's the princess, the heir of Nyambe." The guard turned a wide eye.

"My princess," he bowed in greeting. "This way please," he said, leading the way.

The cave was only a pathway that led to an open space; a hideout. There were hundreds of them; at least two hundred men, excluding women and children. These were the few who had not pledged their allegiance to Masisi and the powers of Buwana.

Initially, they had hidden in caves and bushes, until they found a hideout and formed a small community through the wisdom and strength of Zatanya, the blacksmith.

Malaika pointed to someone coming their way. Atama turned to see a six-foot-tall, well-built man in his early thirties. He had long hair braided into a long ponytail. He had a beautiful face that spoke of untold wisdom and a well-built muscle that suit his structure. He was truly handsome.

Atama stared at him with wonder. The temptation to read his mind was so strong but she was determined to resist it.

"Hello, Malaika," he smiled as he extended his hands in greetings. "I hear you have brought the princess of Malunga and the very heir of Nyambe to us."

Turning to greet Atama, he extended his hand. They held hands for a while before Atama freed her hands, a little embarrassed, hoping her heart would not betray any feeling.

"I hear you have come to recruit an army of the resistance. Well, here we are," gesturing towards the small community.

Atama was excited that she had found them, but perhaps something else gladdened her heart. She thrust the thought away and decided to stay focused and to put up her guards, lest she fell prey once again.

"I shall assemble the camp and we shall take it from there," Zatanya was saying.

"Eh, take what from where?" Atama was not listening. Her eyes were completely focused on his face.

"The mission to begin recruiting the army of the resistance."

Zatanya took Atama on a tour around the camp.

"It's a large crowd," she noticed.

The camp was clean and looked much like a village. They had fresh fruits and the aroma of freshly cooked bush meat consumed the camp. Some women stood in clusters discussing the change that await the camp. Children were consumed with their play while the men sharpened their swords. They stood in awe as Zatanya and Atama toured the camp.

"Let me introduce you to the three tigers," Zatanya pointed to three brothers who bowed courteously with bright smiles.

Atama wondered why they were called tigers because she thought they did not look fierce. She doubted they could hurt a fly.

As if Zatanya could read her thoughts, he said, "don't bother about their looks. There's more to them. This is Bogati, the elephant. He understands and communicates with elephants. But most importantly, he sounds just like them."

Bogati made a loud sound just like the elephant. Atama was amazed.

He smiled shyly and stepped backwards.

"This is Preye," Zatanya continued, "he is a musician. He plays the Sakoma flute."

"Really?"

Atama was amazed. Ruhu had told her about the Sakoma flute, of how the possessor could play to the tune of whatever he wanted in life. He could communicate with nature and also with the hearts of men. As they say, "music is the bread of life." The Sakoma flute was played before and after any battle. Even the sun smiled at the sound of the flute.

"It's an honour to meet you," Atama told Preye with admiration.

"I'm humbled, my princess. It's a shame I'm still a learner, as my father was the true Sakoma flute player. I'm still learning the language of nature," Preye said with a smile.

"Where's your father?" She asked.

"Masisi killed him two years ago," Preye said with a voice of lamentation.

"I'm so sorry," Atama replied in all honesty.

"And finally, meet Mukaba the lion. Every trait of a lion is upon him. He roars like a lion, runs like a lion, has teeth like a lion and also fights like one," Zatanya said.

"Oh really! They sure don't look like one," Atama thought.

Zatanya went on to introduce her to other people in the camp and she noticed that they all had supernatural powers but most of them did not know their full potential or how to use it.

Zatanya addressed the camp about Atama's mission to recruit anyone willing to join the army of resistance.

They were to travel to Amani where they would meet Ruhu the guardian of the Stone Wall of Secret. There, they would be trained physically and their supernatural gifts would be developed. The purpose was to build an army that would fight, conquer Masisi and hold the powers of Buwana captive.

Enlisting was open to everyone, including women and children. No one was too great or feeble to join. The requirement for enlisting was to swear an oath to Nyambe in heart and truth. The recruitment ceremony would begin the following day.

The crowd cheered in excitement as they were dispatched to their tents.

***

As dawn appeared gradually, the sound of the Sakoma flute moved slowly in rhythm with its appearance. One would think the sound controlled the transition from darkness to daybreak. Atama thought that was the sweetest sound she had ever heard. The player sounded skilful as he ushered the dark into the morning. Soon, the camp was awake and gathered before Zatanya's tent, singing and dancing with Preye, the Sakoma flute player leading the proceedings. They sang and danced until smoke filled the camp and dew fell upon the people. The dew was a sign of reassurance that Nyambe was still alive and would one day return to save them from the powers of Buwana.

Zatanya wasted no time and began the recruitment process. With the flute still playing softly, each person came forward and swore allegiance to Nyambe, starting from Zatanya.

"I, Zatanya, today, take an oath to fight the powers of Buwana and to establish the reign of Nyambe, even with the last drop of my blood."

Atama dipped her spear into a ram's blood and placed it on his arm, a sign of initiation and confirmation. As soon as he completed his, he joined Atama, and together, they confirmed everyone taking the oath. In a short while, the entire camp enlisted and took the oath.

That evening, there was a celebration and the Sakoma flute was played. It was a refreshing moment and a sheer privilege to hear the Sakoma song itself being played. The song was only played to Nyambe when seating on his throne. That day, it was sung because the oath was allegiance to him.

The camp was filled with smoke, thunder struck and there was a whirlwind. The people were terrified. Preye's heart was beating fast, wondering why he played the Sakoma song. Everyone thought so too. But then came the dew. It was so heavy like droplets of rain. The camp was quiet and at peace, satisfied that they have been accepted after all.

Zatanya assembled the camp just before nightfall. He said,

"Our first mission is to go back to the city of Malunga and fish out the remnant, so that we may journey back with Princess Atama. We shall strategize, and tomorrow, some of us will go into the city in disguise. Now get some rest. We have a lot to do tomorrow."

Atama admired the charisma and authority Zatanya have over the people, alongside their confidence and respect for him.

"He is indeed a great leader," she thought but that was not the only thought on her mind. How to handle the betrayal of Zuchi and outsmart her was also on her mind. She was bothered that the people might walk right into Masisi and Queen Zuchi's trap.

10

The dancers made their way to the field with numerous waists, and colourful hand and leg beads, well decorated for the ceremony. The fire players were also stationed, as countless magical tricks were showcased. The people of Malunga all gathered as Masisi finally took their princess officially as his bride.

Masisi stood from his skull-made throne and the dancers and crowd quieted.

"The people of Malunga, praise me," he echoed.

"We praise you." They hailed him.

"The people of Malunga, I alone am to be adored," he boasted.

"The powers of Buwana have finally done wonders," he continued. "Now see for yourselves."

With that, the magicians assembled the different algae mixtures and boom! A vision of Nyambe being defeated by Buwana was displayed.

"Ouch!" cried the crowd.

The image revealed their king, the great Nyambe in chains, being dragged and pleading for his life. Disappointment and pain washed through the crowd as the image was taken away.

"Ha ha ha!" Masisi laughed mercilessly.

"Now to crown that defeat, I will be taking your princess as my bride."

Zuchi stood and walked majestically like a queen to stand beside Masisi.

"She's not as foolish as your dead king. She knows how to accept defeat and surrender for her dear life and I think it's wise to emulate her. I present to you your queen, Queen Zuchi of Malunga." The crowd sorrowfully bowed.

That day, agony washed over Malunga, hit with another dose of defeat. All hopes were dashed. First, the defeat of their King Nyambe; now the princess. The people felt their fate was finally sealed with defeat.

Masisi's joy knew no bounds as his plans were taking shape. At night, Zuchi prepared herself for her moment with Masisi. She had also planned on how to be relevant to Masisi, lest he suspects who she truly was. She must display superpowers to remain relevant and stay alive. So, when Masisi came in, she pretended to be in a powerful trance.

"Hmmm! I see them, hmmm!" With her eyes closed, she turned abruptly towards Masisi.

"You must conquer them. The resistance, they are raising an army to defeat you. They camped outside the city." Suddenly she opened her eye, remembering almost all that Princess Atama had told her.

"They will head to Amani," she continued, "through the great River Galana-Sabaki. We must find them now."

Filled with rage and frustration, Masisi roared in anger. "Why are these people stubborn?" he wondered.

***

That evening, Zatanya and Atama, along with ten other men from the camp of the resistance hid in bushes outside of Malunga, patiently awaiting nightfall. As soon as the clouds turned dark, Atama and Zatanya devised a plan, shared the men into two, each of them leading a team, and then headed into the city of Malunga.

Atama instructed them not to use their weapons except in self-defence; they were on a tactical rescue mission. Preye, the Sakoma flute player would remain in the hideout continually playing soft notes that called the people to where he was while the group continued.

Atama disguised herself like a seamstress, as usual, and came to the square where the dancers and drunkards met. She began to read minds but noticed that most of them were discouraged from information passed on to them. She focused on an elderly woman, searching her mind deeply. She tried to read her memory but it was a bit difficult. She must try to have contact with this lady for her to access her thoughts. She made her way towards the woman but nearly got smirched in the head, as the woman reached her apron and brought out a wooden cooking spoon, smashing it on the head of a young boy of about fifteen years.

"Haven't I told you to stop coming out here?"

Taken aback, Atama almost turned with fear to retreat but the tear that escaped the woman's eye caught her attention. She rushed to offer some consolation, putting her hand on the woman's shoulder. She quickly began to search through her mind while she offered kind words of consolation.

The woman's memory revealed the deceitful information dispatched by Masisi earlier, the disappointment and loss of hope from the news about the defeat of King Nyambe. The only hope this woman had, had been stolen. She was frustrated and tired. Two of her children had joined Masisi's army. The only one left had been visiting the inn since the news of the death of King Nyambe. With this advantageous information, Atama knew how to handle the situation. She also perceived that the woman was part of those yet to bow to the powers of Buwana, and many more like her had no hope left because of the deceit of Masisi. Atama realized that they must act fast, lest they saved no one.

"Come Ma'ale. Let's take some air outside."

Touched by Atama's act of kindness, which was rare those days, the woman followed her, with her son coming along.

Atama gave her some water to drink from her side jar. The woman took notice of it, knowing it was only a sojourner that carried such along.

"You're not from this region; are you?" The woman asked her.

Surprised, she wondered if she truly looked different.

"Your water jar looks like that of a sojourner," the woman said again.

"Oh, I have been gone for a while, but I'm back to lighten up the hope of the people of Malunga," Atama responded.

"Hope? How? Our king has suffered a severe defeat. Our hope is gone, dead forever!" The woman lamented.

Atama held the woman's hand and reassured her, "Don't speak much about hope. Have you forgotten that all men are liars and only the words of King Nyambe are true? Nyambe cannot be defeated."

Atama whispered, "I am Princess Atama, the heir to the great King Nyambe."

"Ah!" The woman gasped with her hands in her mouth.

"The princess? It can't be. Zuchi is the princess and the daughter of Nyambe. Everybody knows that. Although it's a sad story now, you do know that she's now the queen of Malunga, the wife of the traitor Masisi?"

Atama's heart was dishevelled. See the damage Zuchi has caused already. Nevertheless, with a determined heart, Atama promised herself to make things right.

"Ma'ale, I am the heir of the great King Nyambe, and Zuchi was my maid. Most people do not know because we look alike in height, and the king made sure our maids were more of friends, someone to talk and play with. That way we would not be lonely, and also not be denied the privilege of growing like normal children. You wouldn't know Zuchi was the maid except you lived in the palace."

Atama went on to relate the story of the attack that day in the Stone Wall of Secret, how her brother, Makundu the prince, was killed and the escape plan by Ruhu before Masisi's web caught them.

The woman listened carefully.

Atama continued,

"Now, we are on a mission to recruit the resistance, those who haven't bowed to the powers of Buwana nor pledged allegiance to Masisi the great deceiver."

"But King Nyambe is dead; we saw him die by the powers of Buwana. Masisi showed it to us," The woman retorted.

"It's a lie. Masisi wants to crush all hopes and gain more powers and allegiance over the people of Malunga," Atama told the woman.

Surprised but full of hope, joy lit the woman's face. She turned to Atama and said to her, "You must come with me. I will introduce you to the others. We should join the resistance." She turned to her son who nodded his head in agreement.

Preye's flute could be heard playing softly. They followed through to the hideout until they located him. Hope filled the woman as she heard and saw the Sakoma flute.

"I must rush back to rescue others," Atama said.

"Wait," the woman called. "I must tell my friends and relatives. They are twenty-five in number and they haven't bowed yet."

"Then come quickly, let us return."

Soon, they were back with several others. Zatanya also arrived with several men and together, they headed for the resistance camp outside Malunga.

It was a joyful celebration that night as more people joined the resistance camp and took their oath of allegiance.

"Tomorrow, we will select some men and go back to Malunga again. We must be very careful, lest we create any form of suspicion."

11

Zuchi was on her way to Kiyambo's quarters. They had been involved in secret affairs. In the corridor, she heard two maids telling each other to hurry. They looked and acted suspiciously. Out of curiosity, she hid and decided to follow them. Slowly, she followed in the dark. The two maids walked fast, looking over their shoulders from time to time, to be sure no one followed them. They listened to the Sakoma music and followed the sound. Zuchi quietly followed behind. Soon they arrived at the hideout and met a crowd waiting for them. They were the last to arrive and they headed straight away for the resistance camp.

Zuchi kept her head ducked in her cape and followed from a long distance. As they were going, Princess Atama stopped.

"I hear movements," she said as she turned abruptly, and there it was, a rabbit escaping into the bush.

"Not so fast," she declared, as she thrust her spear, hitting her target. She fetched the big rabbit and they kept moving.

Zuchi, upon seeing the skill with which Atama hit her target, was gripped with fear. She was not sure it would be wise to keep on. So she stopped at a distance, and luckily, she saw them go through an entrance covered with leaves.

"That must be their hideout," she thought.

Quietly, she retraced her steps and headed back to Malunga.

***

All morning, Masisi and his soldiers kept strategizing on how to identify and track down the resistance. By nightfall, he was frustrated, tired and angry. Masisi came into Zuchi's chamber looking tired and haggard.

"And what might have been troubling you, my love?" She asked, but before he could provide an answer, she busted, "I have good news for you."

"What kind of good news?" Masisi asked, looking indifferent.

"The resistance, I have seen their hideout, and the princess is with them."

"The princess? Which princess?"

Zuchi was dumbfounded. How could she have made such a grave mistake? What a grave mishap!

"Which princess?" Masisi asked again.

"Em, em. The leader of the resistance," Zuchi stammered.

"If she's the princess, then what are you, you bitch?" He took her by her dark braided hair, pulling her roughly until he tucked her head under his armpit.

"You slut, you are the maid," Masisi shook his head.

"Could this be a trick?" Filled with rage, Masisi smashed Zuchi's head on the wall. She gasped for air and fell mute on the floor. He slammed the door in anger, leaving Zuchi half-conscious on the floor.

Hours later, two maids attended to Zuchi in the maids' quarters. When she regained consciousness, she wondered what she was doing in the maids' quarters stripped of her royal apparel. The maids offered her a fresh boiled Zobo drink and a piece of roasted yam. Even though she was full of rage, she took it and devoured it thankfully.

She needed to think fast. Now that Masisi had caught her in her craftiness, she feared that he might demand her head on the stake soon.

"I need to come up with a plan or I lose everything. I must visit Kiyambo this night else, I'm doomed," she told herself.

Back at the camp, Atama stood to address the recruits. She realized that her group had more women and children, with just a couple of men.

"The journey to meet Ruhu is not an easy one," she began. "I admonish us all to be sober and vigilant, because our adversary Masisi, the Mape monkeys, and the powers of Buwana will begin to hunt for our blood; but we must remember that we have pledged our allegiance to Nyambe either in life or death, and he will see us through." The crowd cheered and clapped.

"At every point, Preye the Sakoma flute player will go before us while we match along. Now get some rest, be refreshed for the journey ahead," she concluded.

Princess Atama dismissed the people and found a place to rest, while she reflected on all that had happened and how to strategize for the journey.

Zatanya was speaking to Mukaba the lion, but when he noticed Atama was all by herself, he quickly took the opportunity.

"You're a great leader, you know?"

Atama turned to see the intruder in her private moment.

'Oh, Zatanya! It's you?" she asked.

"You are a lady to be admired," he continued.

"Zatanya, you know I don't do well with flatteries," Atama warned.

"I suppose I'm not flattering you. You are truly incredible; it's a compliment," Zatanya argued.

"If that's the case, I will accept your compliment if only you rephrase your statement by calling me a warrior instead of a lady," she winked with a smile.

"Oh, I see! You have impressed me more as a warrior than just as a lady. My apologies," he said, slightly embarrassed that he was showing too much emotion.

"I have an uneasy feeling. I'm not sure why. I smell doom looming in the atmosphere," Atama confided in Zatanya.

"Hmm, I understand that feeling. I had the same feeling the night before the fall of our beautiful kingdom Malunga. I couldn't sleep and the hair on my armpit kept rising. I didn't know what it meant until the news of the death of Prince Makundu," he said the words soberly, "the disappearance of King Nyambe and the palace. I think whatever you are feeling is real and we must be very careful, else the mission to deliver the resistance to Ruhu be truncated," Zatanya warned.

"We need a plan on how to move the people. You know Masisi will not let us have a smooth journey without a fight. He has a large army and he's obsessed with the powers of Buwana. Also, another dilemma at hand is the betrayal of Zuchi. By now, Masisi ought to have been accurately informed of our plans, if not our hideout," Atama emphasized.

"Hmm! I see your concerns." Zatanya put a finger on his chin, thinking for a while. "I think I have a plan," he said.

***

A maid had just sneaked out of Kiyambo's chambers. Zuchi was exasperated as she walked in.

"Kiyambo, for goodness' sake, give me some respect. Knowing that I'd be visiting you, must you lay with a maid before my arrival?" Zuchi queried.

"Ah!, my queen, you're here!" he replied sarcastically. "Have no worries. Kiyambo is sufficient for all," he winked devilishly at her.

"You look troubled. Now, what can I do for you, besides…" Kiyambo said, looking at her body seductively.

He pulled her into his arms, revealing his shirtless body, especially his chest and arms.

"Kiyambo, this can wait, please. I need to speak with you. There's fire on the mountain," Zuchi cried.

"You mean your mountain," he corrected.

"Yeah, whatever. Look, Masisi has found out," Zuchi broke the news.

"Found out what? That you're an ordinary maid and not the Princess?" Kiyambo gave quaky laughter.

"Kiyambo, this is not funny. You need to help me, else my head will be hanging on the stake," Zuchi pleaded.

"Zuchi Zuchi, why should I help you? Why should I care if Masisi takes off your head?" Kiyambo retorted.

Zuchi was surprised by his response. All this while, she thought Kiyambo loved her. At least she thought he cared about her. It was beginning to dawn on her that in Masisi's reign and kingdom, it was purely a matter of survival of the fittest.

"To stay alive, you must play the game to live or you die and that's game over for you," she thought.

"You have to help me, else Masisi will have your head too," she insisted in an angry tone.

"How could you be the guard in charge of Ruhu, Atama and myself and not know who the real princess is? He will assume you were part of our plans all along. As for me, I will tell him about our love affair. I will tell him you raped me and forced me to keep quiet else you would reveal my true identity," Zuchi threatened.

Kiyambo's eyes turned red. The thought of strangling her to death consumed his mind. He could do it very fast, but on a second note, he decided to play along.

"So, what's your plan?" He asked her.

"Better choice," she responded before going on to tell him her plans.

"You will help me get to Masisi's chamber this night. You know there's no way I can get to him without your help; the guards will never let me in since they know I'm now a prisoner," she explained.

"So, when you get there, what are you going to say or do?" He asked.

"The resistance, I know all about them and their hideout. I will plead with him to let me take him and the soldiers there. I will also blackmail him into keeping me alive. Since the people think I'm the princess of Malunga, he must leave it that way. If he reveals that I'm just the maid and that the princess and Ruhu are alive, that will give them a flicker of hope and may raise some doubt about his vision of killing King Nyambe. I will intimidate him to allow me to help him catch the resistance and also keep the hopes of the people destroyed."

"Hmm! I see you have thought this quite well. So, when do you want to see him?"

"I suppose this night, else it will be too late when we arrive at their hideout."

That night, Zuchi dressed like one of the maidens that shared the bed with Masisi. With the help of Kiyambo, she found her way to the bed of Masisi, waiting for him to come in.

When he noticed she was the one, he turned to send for the guards.

"Hear me out before you act rashly Masisi. I have good news for you and a proposal," Zuchi said quickly, to draw his attention.

She told him everything. He thought it through, realizing that the benefit of keeping the lie was far greater to achieving his mission than having her head chopped off.

The next day, Zuchi was reinstalled as the queen of Malunga. That night, Masisi assembled a hundred soldiers.

"We will have a quick raid and capture the resistance."

Masisi gave specific instructions that Atama be captured alive. He will ensure she is tortured until she reveals Ruhu's whereabouts. Then Ruhu also would be captured. Together, they would fetch him the signet ring of King Nyambe. That way, with the help of the powers of Buwana, Nyambe would be invoked back from the unknown; Buwana's two sons would be free, while King Nyambe's children, Atama and Makundu, would replace his sons in the bottle. Buwana would defeat good forever, putting Nyambe in the same bottle as his children.

Masisi was pleased with his plans and was sure of his victory.

"The raid will be quick and fast," he thought.

12

The night before the raid, Masisi invoked the presence of Buwana. He chanted all day and night. Pools of animals' blood were shed for sacrifice to ensure victory. He chanted until the blood gushed from his nostrils and eyes. One of the soldiers had to pull him from the chant for the powers were almost consuming him. Being filled with dark powers, Masisi released an enclosed bottle. A green and brown smoke, having the form of an alligator, evaporated into the outer part of Malunga. The smoke-like creature fell on the trees, and the grass, and filled the atmosphere, such that the cloud held a strange presence of doom.

Now the soldiers were armed and ready. Zuchi, all dressed in seductive apparel with a zebra cape over her body, rode on the horse beside Masisi, while the soldiers matched on foot, as she led the way to the hideout of the resistance.

***

Princess Atama turned and tossed in her straw bed. Suddenly, she heard footsteps. Before she could comprehend the situation, and with no time to alert the others, the entire village was set on fire. The atmosphere was full of dread and fear.

The men holding weapons were too afraid to use them. She noticed they would not even run. She shouted to them to run, but they seemed not to hear her. She saw some children standing with their gaze on the sky. She beckoned on them to hide, but they would not move. The feeling of frustration washed over her. She felt sick and tired.

In a twinkle of an eye, an arrow hit her back, sending her to her knees. Within a few seconds, her mouth was tied with a dirty scarlet rope. Her hands were bound and she noticed that movement was difficult for her. She checked her feet and noticed a smoky green-like object forming a chain around her feet. She looked closely and noticed the object was like a living creature. It was alive and breathing.

Atama then looked closely at the feet of the others, the children and the men with their weapons, and it dawned on her that the same smoky creature that bound her feet had also chained the feet of others. Then she heard a familiar voice;

"Fear. This is the spirit of fear. Fear will disarm the people and make them surrender without a fight."

Atama awoke from the disheartening dream, checking her feet and rubbing them together. She could still feel the strands of fear looming in the atmosphere. Feeling a sense of urgency, she crawled out of her bed and found Zatanya in the dark. The camp was dark and gloomy.

"Zatanya!" She whispered in the dark, "The enemy is here; can you hear them?"

"No, I can't. Did you see someone?" He whispered back.

"No, but they are here already. We must assemble the people and give them the information beforehand. Fear is worse than a legion of the army and it's here already in the camp."

Now Zatanya understood what she implied. With fear in the camp already, defeat was almost inevitable. Quickly, he signalled Preye to play the Sakoma flute, ushering everyone to assemble.

Soon the people gathered. Atama stood to address them. The people looked full of dread and like a blanket of uncertainty had clasped around them. One could feel the pungent smell of fear so thick like a cloud, oozing out of them.

"We have no time left. We must move this night. However, we must tread with care. The enemy is in the camp already and the battle has begun. You must conquer the fear in your heart. See, Masisi has evoked the foul spirit called fear and that spirit is false and merciless. It does not show mercy to its captives. It has only one mission, to defeat."

As she spoke, her words were like a healing balm that began to set the people free. When Atama saw the effect her words had on the congregation, she signalled to Preye and he began to play something very soft that spoke about war and victory, as she continued to extol the people.

"You must believe that you are conquerors that cannot be defeated. Our mission is to get to Amani, and Amani we shall reach with your lives intact because the spirit of Nyambe goes with us. Though you cannot see him, he will help us get to Amani. With the last drop of our blood, we will fight, if need be, but we must all get to Amani."

The people looked robust, filled with the encouragement to forge on.

"We move!" Atama ordered.

The people began to pack whatever little belongings they could gather. The women and children moved in groups and the company of a few men. Atama and Bogati the elephant moved ahead, while Zatanya, Preye and Mukaba the lion lingered behind. All through,

Preye kept playing the flute while the people marched on.

They marched in silence for hours in between trees and dried bushes. The atmosphere still carried doom. By dawn, they had covered a reasonable distance from the camp but still had three days' journey ahead of them before they could get to Amani.

By morning, Masisi and the soldiers had arrived at the camp. They invaded, only to find the camp empty. However, the place looked like it was once inhabited.

"They are gone," Masisi hissed "but they couldn't have gone far."

So he commanded the soldiers to proceed after them.

They marched on and in no time, they could see them from afar. Masisi was ready for war. Heading for his mission, he commanded his troops to launch an attack.

The first arrow hit a woman on the leg.

"Masisi is here," the others screamed, taking off for dear lives.

The people were hysterical and all began to run. Atama alerted Bogati to take charge while she lingered to fight with the men. Bogati whistled for the arrival of his ancestors, the Bogandi elephants. With a loud match, they arrived, a hundred of them. Soon the women and children rode the Bogandi elephants. Masisi's soldiers were advancing. Zatanya and Mukaba were in the defence position. Atama joined them, along with some men. They fought mercilessly.

The battle was becoming fierce. Atama and her team had to retreat. They needed another plan; or else Masisi would capture the entire camp. Atama needed to meet with Bogati to lead the way to Amani. She needed to think very fast. Mukaba ushered the lions he commanded, expecting the lions to arrive in multitude just like the Bogandi elephants.

Mukaba roared like a lion but no lion appeared. However, the battle almost stopped as the ground shook and the wind carried the sound of the roar to the ends of the earth, taking some of Masisi's soldiers along, smashing them among trees and rocks.

"Impressive," Atama thought "but where are the other lions?" She demanded.

Mukaba had not learned the full skill of summoning more lions. Besides, only three lions could appear at a time. Mukaba had not developed the ability to call them or to control them, lest they ate everybody.

There was little time to learn more about the lions. They needed another plan, or else they would all be finished. Atama ran off the battleground. She found a place and began to call out to Ruhu but not until an arrow went through her arm. She fell flat on the dirt as Masisi and Zuchi approached her.

13

"Now look who we have here," Masisi was looking down at Atama's motionless body. She had suffered a severe blow and lay lifeless on the ground. Zatanya and the others were still fighting courageously, not knowing what had happened until someone from the resistance screamed that the princess had been taken.

"What!" Zatanya was confused.

How could that be? What would he do? There was no time to think or plan. One thing was certain, to flee. He began to call the others to take cover. He, Bogati and Preye, with the help of the elephants, were able to hide in caves, although a number of the resistance was captured.

The resistance had the advantage of surviving in the bush. They used several camouflages as cover, away from the soldiers in search of them.

Women and children were taken away along with Atama. Masisi was pleased with the mission, and the advantage Zuchi gave them. She gallivanted herself with pride in the camp. This was a plus for her. With that, she was certain of her survival and the approval of Masisi. Looking at Atama on the ground, with hands and feet tied, still unconscious, she felt sorry for her.

"Well, I feel sorry for you girl, but I have to do what I need to do to stay alive. It's the survival of the fittest out here," she said to Atama's motionless body and walked away.

The camp smelled of dread and the women and children wondered if anyone could rescue them from the hands of Masisi. Some silently prayed that the princess was still alive. They were all in great fear. The green-like creature had once again crept into the camp and had bound the people's hands and feet. It was so thick one could see and feel it. The atmosphere was subdued by the green colouration of doom.

When it was nightfall, Zatanya, Bogati and Preye assembled to devise a rescue plan. Malaika came along. She thought it was a suicidal mission but urged them to go on. She would stay with the few in her company, and if they had to fight, they would fight to the death instead of being captured and taken back as prisoners.

A few hours into the night, one could see four soldiers on duty, while the others tried to catch some sleep. The campfire was almost out. Princess Atama was still unconscious. By this time, everyone feared she might die in her sleep. Hours earlier, Masisi cursed and threatened her not to even think of dying. He needed her alive. She would be of no use to him if she died. He made sure she was in a comfortable condition while they waited for her to regain consciousness.

Zatanya quietly sneaked into the camp with Bogati. Preye was on the watch. He thought of how to distract the guards without exposing their cover. While they were still contemplating, a straying rabbit made a noisome movement around their hideout and all four soldiers turned towards the direction with a burning firestick.

"Who goes there?" they called, carrying their weapons along.

"Run!" Zatanya shouted as he narrowly escaped a stray arrow.

In a few minutes, the entire camp was awake, getting prepared for defence.

Princess Atama blinked as the noise increased, and her eyes opened. Still not fully aware of her environment, she tried to move but found she could not.

"Help" was all she could mutter and slept back.

Then suddenly, she found herself bound hand and foot with a thicket. She was cold, tired and hungry. She could hear the cry of a helpless baby not so far away. She tried desperately to free herself so she could help the baby, but each time she tried to let loose, the ropes got tighter. In frustration, she cried for help, only to turn and, in great surprise, he was standing close to her.

Ruhu was standing all along beside her. She was happy to see him. She had a lot to ask him but that was not the right time. Of course, he could read her mind but did not respond.

Some minutes passed before he spoke with such urgency and authority.

"Let me reveal the greatest weapon within you," he began. "It's not a canal weapon, but strong and mighty. It can bring down principalities, power, wickedness in high places, evil imaginations and intentions. Most importantly, it's able to set you free."

By now Ruhu's eyes had turned red and at his last word, Atama burst out chanting incantations, speaking in an unknown tongue and emitting fire from her mouth. A loud noise like the rumbling of waters filled the atmosphere and the ropes in her hands let loose. The thicket shattered into tiny sticks. Surprised but happy, she chanted on with power.

In the process, Atama regained consciousness, while still chanting the incantations.

Zatanya and Bogati who were already captured and bound, watched in awe as Atama fired on incantations.

"Zhatamarabatazeteribababababarokorimbatazarakab otabobobobloblibrokotayimbo," and on she went, releasing physical arrows in hundreds from her mouth, which pierced the soldiers. When they tried to shoot at her, a strange force shielded her and their gunpowder dashed to the ground.

Soon, Zatanya and Bogati were free from their bonds and they began to fight along Atama. Preye saw the battle, took his Sakoma and began to play. The sound was amplified miraculously. The soldiers could hear and see legions of armies marching towards them.

"Flee! Flee!" They cried to one another.

Masisi recognized the strange power. Nyambe was fighting for them. He took to his heels and the moment he got a grip of his fingers, he pressed his signet ring and disappeared. Zuchi turned and realized she was alone. So, she snatched a baby from its mother's hand to use as a shield for escape, pointing a pocket knife at the baby's side.

Atama turned to her, "You don't want to do this," she said.

With all her anger, she took her spear and sent it straight into Zuchi's brain, while Preye swiftly caught the baby before she hit the ground.

Atama looked upon the lifeless body of Zuchi and said, "Vanity upon vanity, for whatsoever a man sows, that shall he reap." She spat and walked away.

Soon, the people gathered in excitement. They were complete in number. Except for a few injuries, they were all alive. They sang and danced as they continued their journey.

In two days, they arrived at the great River Galana-Sabaki. The people were happy. The crocodiles scanned the group to ascertain their purity. They harmlessly transported them over to Amani where Ruhu, the great keeper of the Stone Wall of Secret awaited them.

With a big smile, Atama ran into the embrace of her teacher, keeper, and best friend Ruhu. He held her for a moment.

"I'm proud of you," he whispered into her ears. "You have done well and your father, the great King Nyambe, is proud of you." Atama could not help but blush.

"Thank you, Ruhu," she said.

Ruhu turned to the crowd and said, "I greet you, the great and mighty men of valour. You have fought a good fight and have stood by the truth."

He went round the crowd, greeting and shaking hands with everyone.

"Please come, eat, drink and rest."

Ruhu took them to a beautiful site with wildflowers, fountain and bush berries, where he had prepared picnic mats in different groups with fire, sticks and jars of water. They sat in groups, lighted the fires and began roasting the rabbits Ruhu handed to them. They ate, drank and made merry. At last, they were safe from fear and evil, but it was for a while, as evil lay out there and they must train to fight and defeat the powers of Buwana.

***

Zatanya found Atama by the fountain. The wind blew her hair, carrying it lazily like winnowed chaff. He stood for a while, admiring her.

"She's beautiful, strong, courageous and a true leader," he thought.

"Greetings to you Princess Atama the great warrior," Zatanya hailed her.

She turned with a sweet smile. "Thank you Zatanya, greetings to you too."

He came and stood beside her. They were watching an elephant give birth from a distance. She had struggled for hours, maybe days even, but finally gave birth.

"You know, the struggles of life are like this," she turned to face him. "The struggles and troubles are hard but they are meant to birth something beautiful at the end of the day."

Zatanya took her hand. "Something as beautiful as these hands," he said.

"No, that's not what I was thinking. I meant something as beautiful as our victory" she corrected but they both knew exactly what they meant for their heart spoke of beautiful love.

Atama placed her hands in his and smiled. Ruhu came over to share a plan with her about their next move, but when he saw the two locking hands, he quietly stepped back with a broad smile on his face.

"Today is to enjoy and appreciate the gift of love, while tomorrow is to get on with the plans and activities of ensuring the return of Nyambe."

ABOUT THE AUTHOR

Nissih is an incredible storyteller, with ancestral roots in Nigeria, Africa. She is best known for her deep, rich and compelling African stories narrated in an intriguing and compelling way that leaves her readers glued to their books.

She has a degree in Mass Communications from Ahmadu Bello University, a PGD in Education (NTI) and a Certificate in Creative Writing. She's an avid reader, loves historical movies and of recently has begun to explore script writing. She also writes literature suitable for Primary and Secondary schools.

www.ingramcontent.com/pod-product-compliance
Lightning Source LLC
LaVergne TN
LVHW050546160826
845677LV00011B/2200

* 9 7 9 8 3 7 0 5 1 3 2 7 5 *